The Emerald Bottle

Book 1

Linda Shields Allison

Published by BookLocker.com, Inc., St. Petersburg, Florida.

Printed on acid-free paper.

The characters and events in this book are fictitious. Any similarity to real persons, living or dead, is coincidental and not intended by the author.

BookLocker.com, Inc.
2020

First Edition

Library of Congress Cataloging in Publication Data
Allison, Linda Shields
The Emerald Bottle by Linda Shields Allison
Library of Congress Control Number: 2020908720

For my 100% Irish American
Mom who was the inspiration
for this book.

Acknowledgements ~

Russell Mars who encouraged me to finish the trilogy. You were by my side every step of the way. You are my heart.

Claudia Weston for her joyful enthusiasm, steadfast encouragement and support. You were the first to have faith in my story and inspired me from the beginning.

Terry Nettles Meaney for her extraordinary skill in editing my work.

Illean Graves Trautwein who offered invaluable literary advice and affirmation.

Mike and Tina Canon for their brilliant technical support and creative talent.

Roy and Lynette Warren for driving me all over Ireland in search of my roots.

Rudy and Norma Romero for their amazing marketing skills in promoting the books.

My family ~ the infinite joy in my life that makes me most proud.

My Dad, Bruce Shields, and brother Mike. I know you watched over me as spiritual guides on this literary journey.

The Journey of the Bottle Trilogy
by Linda Shields Allison

The Emerald Bottle

The Bronze Bottle

The Amethyst Bottle

The Characters ~

Tara Maguire: Forced to pay off a family debt to Squire Dellamort, twelve-year-old Tara is indentured to his estate for one year. The squire reneges on a written promise to pay Tara's passage in steerage by contriving a plot that falsely accuses her of stealing. Tara flees the estate with her little dog, Bailey, and with the help of a family of Irish Tinkers and a mysterious Emerald Bottle struggles to reunite with her family.

Michael and Elsie Maguire: The potato crop fails, and Tara's parents lose their five-acre farm when they cannot make the mortgage payments to Dellamort Bank. The family immigrates to Prince Edward Island, Canada, but must leave their daughter in Ireland.

Grandma Cassie: Tara's grandma must sell her beloved Belleek pitcher and bowl to the second-hand shop for money during the Potato Famine. She declines on the voyage to Canada from ship fever, but her special influence guides Tara through a difficult year alone.

Squire Chase Dellamort: The spoiled squire spends his days, on the estate he inherited from his father, giving lavish parties, riding his horse, and gambling. Indifferent to the plight of his many Irish tenant farmers, he evicts those who cannot produce. His abnormal desire to win, and his hatred for Michael Maguire compel the squire and his butler to track Tara to Dublin so they can force her back into servitude on his estate.

Nevil Hawkins: When Tara sees Grandma Cassie's Belleek pitcher and bowl on a table in the butler's office, she is saddened to discover that he purchased it at the second-hand shop. The cruel butler oversees the servants of Dellamort Manor. He is a willing ally in the scheme to frame Tara for stealing.

Shauna Curran: Tara's loyal friend works as a servant on the estate. She learns to read and write from Tara. Shauna exposes the butler's favorite servant, Mary Tully, who is asked to betray Tara as a witness to the phony theft.

Danny Kelly: The shy stable-boy harbors secret feelings for Shauna. Danny and Shauna help Tara flee the estate, then travel to Dublin, with a band of Tinkers, to warn Tara that the squire is pursuing her.

Diviña: Leader of a family of Tinkers, Diviña has been blessed with the gift of second-sight. Diviña finds John Corcoran on the streets of Dublin when he is seven and raises him as her only child. She passes a beautiful bottle into Tara's keeping when it mysteriously changes colors. The curious Emerald Bottle helps Tara on her journey.

John Corcoran: Sixteen-year-old John finds Tara left for dead in the woods and carries her to his Diviña's caravan. At the request of his mother, he reluctantly agrees to help Tara on her journey to Dublin. In time, he comes to appreciate Tara's courage and kindness.

Jack Harte: The Dublin innkeeper assists Diviña in chasing off the group of hooligans who are caught beating the life out of a homeless street urchin. Together, they nurse the young John back to health. Jack becomes a lifelong friend to the Tinkers. He helps Tara find passage on a ship to New Brunswick.

Captain Joshua Scott: Captain Scott owes a debt of gratitude to Jack Harte. The captain agrees to take Tara and her friends to New Brunswick on his sailing ship, the Lisa Renee, but only as a personal favor to Jack Harte.

Preface

Throughout most of its history, many countries invaded a small island, west of England and north of Spain, called Ireland. The most recent trespassers have been the English. From 1695 until 1829, the British imposed harsh Penal Laws upon the Irish people. No Irish could practice the Roman Catholic religion. They were forced off their land and barred from purchasing land, until barely five percent remained in Catholic ownership. Irish Catholics could not vote, hold political office, practice law, carry a gun or a sword, or own a horse worth more than seven dollars. Their children were banned from going to school. Those who wanted to learn to read met, in secret, at outdoor Hedge Schools taught by priests. The system left the Irish paupers in their own land. The British finally repealed the legislation in 1829—sixteen years before a devastating period which came to be known as the *Potato Famine*.

Between the years 1846 to 1851, terrible troubles swept across Ireland causing the worst disaster in Irish history. During this time, half of all Irish lived on small farms, or were tenant farmers on large British-owned estates. The Irish raised cattle and grew grain to pay their rents and other expenses. This left them with only their potato crops to use for food. When a mysterious blight destroyed their potato crops, nearly one million men, women, and children died of starvation and disease. So many people perished, they were buried in mass graves. Countless desperate victims became so hungry they ate grass and became known as the *green mouths*. During these years, hundreds of thousands of Irish citizens left their beloved

Emerald Isle. Forced off their land, they left behind the country they cherished because they had no other choice. The immigrants survived horrible conditions to come by ships in steerage to North America. My ancestors were among the many Irish who came to North America looking for a dream—hoping for a better life.

Prologue ~ July 1845

At County Cavan, Ireland a modest village named Cootehill lay nestled within soft green hills about thirty miles from Dundalk Bay by the Irish Sea. Twenty-four hundred people inhabited the village, which contained a Catholic Chapel and a Protestant Church. Most of the villagers were farmers. A few owned small farms, but most worked as tenant farmers for large estates called plantations. Life was hard for many people, but the village of Cootehill proudly boasted one brewery, two banks, and three pubs. The people collectively ran one of the finest markets in the county. Flax, linen, vegetables, and cattle were among the items briskly traded and sold on market day. In the village there lived a budding lass of ten, named Tara Kathleen Maguire. This story belongs to her.

"Bailey, stop diggin' up the cabbage! 'Tis a dog you are, laddy, not a mole," called Tara. The small black and white dog trotted out of the girl's garden. Bailey squatted on his haunches to stare at the girl pulling weeds near a row of carrots. The little male dog was similar in size to a small fox, and weighed a stone, or the equivalent of fourteen pounds. He had fluffy thick fur, and a small round face. Bailey's black pug nose and large brown eyes gave the dog an impish look. A wispy patch of fur, which fell irreverently from the forehead, sometimes hid the eyes. The dog was not a pedigree but he was smart, and Tara loved him with all her heart.

"Look Bailey, I found a shamrock nestled amongst the weeds. You know, legend has it, that Saint Patrick, our patron saint of Ireland, once explained the Trinity to the people by

15

comparing the three leaves of the shamrock to the Father, the Son, and the Holy Ghost." remarked Tara. "Saint Patrick was a very clever man." Bailey cocked his head, as if he understood every word the girl had uttered. At that moment a rabbit poked its head out of a bush, and Bailey darted off in chase. "Hey, I'm not done with my preaching, laddy." Tara sat back on her heels and laughed. "I hope St. Patrick had better luck with his flock."

Humming to herself, Tara smiled and looked lovingly at her father tending his crops in the distance. Michael Maguire labored long hours each day to produce the barley, oats, flax, and potatoes on his five acres of land. Tara loved to watch her Da toil in his fields.

Tara knew how proud Michael was that *his* family owned the land they worked. He often told Tara how sorry he felt for the many villagers who worked as tenant farmers on the bigger estates. "The husbands, wives, and children who work these rented plots of land are hollow-eyed and hungry. As hard as they work, these families never seem to get ahead. They live hand to mouth." Tara shared his despair. When they took their grain to market, they saw hoards of raggedly clothed children playing barefoot by the road.

"The land, 'tis everything," Michael said time and time again. "Robbie, Joseph, Tara, are you listening to me?. A man without land is a man with no future. To own your land is the key to owning your own life."

"Yes, Da, we know, Da, 'tis the truth, Da," the children always intoned. They had heard the gospel of the land many times before.

Tara had a wild spirit, and was happiest when she could hike and explore the woodlands and meadows. She had a scientific mind and knew the names of all the plants and herbs in the area. She kept meticulous diaries on the local vegetation, and the healing properties of various herbs. The garden she so skillfully tended produced essential food for the table. Tara strived to increase the bounty of her harvest using new farming methods from a book on gardening, which was a gift from her parents for her tenth birthday.

Tara knew she was strong. She could carry a twenty-pound sack of oats to market without effort. She knew a lot about her strength of body and character, but what Tara *didn't* know, was that she was blooming into a rare Irish beauty. Tara was as lovely as a crisp spring morning. From her father, she had inherited a crop of thick curly hair as black and shiny as a raven's feather, and blue eyes that sparkled like the waters of the Irish Sea. Tara's skin was soft and fair, with just a spray of freckles dotting her cheeks and nose. Tara loved her freckles.

Grandma Cassie often said, "Ah, Tara, those with true Celtic blood running in their veins have freckles somewhere on their person. Be proud of your freckles, lass. 'Tis your Irish heritage. 'Tis who you are."

Tara's beauty shined from within. When she wasn't helping the family carve out a living on the farm, she helped all others who came within her radiant circle. Folks often knew Tara was near long before they saw her. They warmed to the familiar sweet tones of a voice raised in song almost every waking moment of the day. Tara sang the same lilting songs that every Irish man, woman, and child knows by heart. She sang the Irish ballads that told the stories of their past.

Ten-year-old Tara Kathleen Maguire lived with her family on a small farm northeast of the village of Cootehill, near Dellamort Forest. Her family's land rested in the shadow of a large tenant estate owned by Squire Chase Dellamort. The squire was the richest man in County Cavan, and Dellamort Manor was the biggest estate in the area. Besides owning most of the land in the county, Dellamort possessed a large brewery, one bank, and one small linen factory. For all that the squire owned, he was not a contented man. He hated riding his horse to the edge of Dellamort Wood only to see Michael Maguire tending his crops on five acres of prime land. The squire coveted Maguire's land.

Tara shared a small thatched cottage with Grandma Cassie, her parents Elsie and Michael, the seven-year-old twins, Robert and Joseph, and her new baby sister, Diane, who was almost two months old. Two other little angels, born in between the twins and Diane, had died in infancy. The Maguire cottage, though small and simple, was polished to a shine every day. The home celebrated the love and pride of a family who labored long hours each day to nourish the land they cherished so dearly.

The kitchen was the heart of the home, and it contained an oak table. Michael had felled the ancient oak tree from his land. With painstaking patience, he dried, sawed, and crafted the oak into a spiritual center, which would bring his family together and share the blessings from the earth. A huge fireplace warmed the kitchen in winter and served as both oven and stove. Cassie and Elsie were wonderful cooks. Grandma Cassie's Irish soda bread was the best in Cootehill, and she had seven blue ribbons from the village fair to prove that it was so. Elsie could serve potatoes in thirty different ways - each as tasty as the next.

When Elsie's father, Papa Frank, had died four winters ago, Grandma Cassie came to live with the family. She and Tara shared a meager room at the back of the cottage where they slept in Cassie's feather bed. Wooden pegs attached to the wall held their few items of clothing. A lovely cream-colored pitcher and bowl, resting on a small table in the corner, were the prettiest things in the room. The delicate porcelain was a present from Papa Frank and Cassie cherished the gift with all her heart.

"Granny, tell me about your beautiful china again?" begged Tara. "No wait, I think I remember. Papa Frank's brother worked in the bleak factory, and he made it special for Papa Frank to give you as your bride's gift when you got married."

"No, child, Papa Frank's brother made it at the *Belleek* factory. But you're right 'twas made especially for our wedding day. 'Tis one of a kind, Tara. There's no other exactly like it," boasted Cassie proudly. "Papa Frank cherished it then, as much as I do today."

"I love to look at it when you wash it in the kitchen," said Tara. "When the sunlight shines on the bowl, I can see the shadow of your hands through the other side. 'Tis like a pair of angel wings shimmering in the glow of a halo."

"Sure, and 'tis a miracle that it hasn't been broken or cracked. Imagine something so fine and fragile lastin' all these many years." Cassie sighed wistfully.

Elsie, Michael, and baby Diane shared the other bedroom located on the east end of the cottage. It was the only room with a large window. Elsie said she never tired of looking outside to see productive fields, Tara's vegetable garden, and a small creek that meandered through their property. She said the window was a living portrait of the seasons of her life. Robbie and Joseph slept in a small loft built above the kitchen. There was no parlor, but Michael had plans to expand when he could set aside some extra cash from the harvests. What the small cottage lacked in grandeur, it made up in warmth. The Maguire home radiated love.

Like the cottage, the farm possessed a sturdy little barn with walls of sod two feet thick. The sod kept the barn warm in the winter and cool in the summer. A ladder led to a small loft filled with hay. The thatched-roof barn smelled of moist earth and hay mingled with the various scents of the animals that dwelled within. It was home to one milking cow named Mrs.

Mooney, two lazy hogs called Buddy and Bonnie, one rooster, and six hens.

Life on the farm was hard, but Tara knew that her family was luckier than most of their neighbors. Each night, as Tara said her prayers, she appealed her patron saint. "Saint Catherine, thank you for watching over our family. Keep us safe and protected. Help the people of our village to grow in the love of our Father. Amen."

Tara looked with pride at her garden as she gathered her gardening tools into her basket. "Bailey, called Tara, 'tis time to help Granny Cassie make the soda bread for the bake sale at Saint Michael's. Bailey, where are you?" After a few minutes, Tara picked up her basket and walked up the path to the cottage. She knew that Bailey would show up in his own sweet time The dog seemed to possess the nature of his mistress. He was trusting and inquisitive and possessed a love of nature.

A few miles to the west of the Maguire cottage, Squire Chase Dellamort sat in his morning room, which faced the southern portion of his estate. Although the pale twenty-nine-year-old was slightly stooped and had rapidly thinning hair the color of dull wet hay, he was still considered the catch of the county by the ladies. The most astonishing feature, about the squire, was his eyes. His left eye was a pasty shade of blue, while the right one was hazel spotted with tiny flecks of mustard-yellow. It was often whispered behind his back, that the flecks in his right eye seemed to change into odd shades of yellow when he became agitated. At that moment, the squire was in a particularly foul temper after losing at a late night poker game.

He barked at his new kitchen servant, Shauna Curran, for spilling a drop of raspberry jam on the lacy white Irish linen napkin that covered his beautiful silver tray. "Who are you? Where's Mary? Get out of my sight you idiot peasant!" The petrified kitchen maid backed out of the room apologizing profusely. Shauna could not believe her careless mistake. She needed this job, and could ill-afford to anger his lordship.

As Squire Dellamort absently nibbled on his toast and drank his Earl Gray tea, he questioned why his butler, Nevil, had hired such a stupid girl in the first place. "Why is proper help so difficult to come by?" he bellowed to the empty room. At that moment his butler, Nevil Hawkins, entered the room with Squire Dellamort's newspaper. At the squire's insistence, the newspaper was ironed daily. He felt that its pages were infected with the same putrid dampness that seemed to settle on everything in this dreadful island. Squire Dellamort was glad that he had just spent three months in the south of France. *To escape is the only way any sane person can endure this abominable climate*, he reflected as he watched his butler walk toward him.

"Good morning, sir," greeted Nevil. I trust that you had a pleasant night's sleep?" Nevil placed the newspaper on the table next to the silver tray with small delicate hands, which looked more like a girl's than any man who had ever done a decent day's work in a field. The butler was a small wiry man with graying hair and steel gray eyes that darted everywhere. Nothing escaped Nevil's vision. The large sharp nose protruding from his face gave him the appearance of a hawk in search of a good meal. Like the hawk, Nevil was a predator. He never missed an opportunity to advance his immediate self-interest.

"No, I didn't have a pleasant night's sleep," mocked the squire in childish tones. He added angrily, "I don't like losing at cards to that fat toad, Lord Higgins! And where did you find that useless serving girl?"

"I will fire her at once, sir, if that is your desire," said Nevil, "but it is my hope that you might see fit to give the girl another chance. She is the daughter of your deceased tenant worker, Dennis Curran. The family is pathetically needy. I believe that the villagers would take it as a noble gesture to help the family by gracing the girl with employment."

"I could give a fiddler's hoot what the village people think of me," shouted the squire. "However," he relented, "I suppose you're right, and I like the fact that she's needy. *Needy* makes an employee bend more easily to the will of the master," he smirked.

"I couldn't agree with you more, sir," said Nevil. "Now, if there is no further need of me, sir, I will leave you to your tea and newspaper." Nevil closed the doors to the morning room softly, smiling that he had steered the conversation as he wanted.

Chase Dellamort picked up the newspaper, but couldn't concentrate enough to read. Absently, he looked around the room. The morning room was one of his favorite rooms in the mansion. It favored five large windows framed in oak, which overlooked one of the three lakes that lay scattered across his estate. The land was rich with meadows and rolling hills. Resting at the highest point of his land stood his beautiful brick mansion. It had been called one of the finest examples of Palladian architecture in all of Europe and had been in his family for nearly one hundred years. It was a shining archetype of the grace that symbolized a man of wealth and stature. To the east of his property stood Dellamort Wood, one of the most beautiful forests in all of Ireland. He loved to ride his black stallion, Rogue, through its dark shady interior. He reveled in the fact that he could ride for hours and never reach the end of his vast estate. That is, until he came to that pitiable little excuse for a farm owned by Michael Maguire and his ample family. The squire scowled just thinking of it, and anyone who might have walked into the room at that moment would have seen the speckles in his right eye spark a menacing shade of amber.

For years, Dellamort had tried to press the Maguire family into selling their land to him. *But, no matter how many offers I've made, or how many secret schemes I've conspired, the wretched family has avoided all my plots to transmit their pathetic pimple of earth into my keeping,* the squire bitterly mused. It annoyed Chase deeply, that although his family had been successful in gathering land from most of the people in the area, he could not add the Maguire's paltry bit of acreage to his holdings. "I will not fail! So far the man has been lucky," voiced the squire out loud. *But if I'm patient, the changing tide of fortune will favor me. Patience is a virtue that can easily be practiced by a rich man. One slip and that trivial parcel of land will be mine.*

Squire Dellamort settled more comfortably into his favorite Chippendale chair and eyed his breakfast with a bit more enthusiasm. *After all, if I'm riding later in the day, I shall need to be well-fortified with food.*

Shauna Curran nervously polished a silver candlestick as Nevil entered the kitchen. "You careless dolt," shouted the butler. "If not for me, the squire would have sent you packing."

The cruel butler grabbed Shauna by the arm and pulled her close to his face. Squeezing her flesh with a steady pressure he growled, "You will do as I tell you, or you will be unemployed. Do you understand what I am saying?"

Shauna had never known such terror in her life. She wanted to run out of the mansion and home to her mother, but she knew that would be folly. She needed this job to help support her family and had to make it work. In a voice that shook with terror she uttered, "I promise. 'Twill not happen again, sir. Please, Mr. Hawkins, you're hurting my arm."

Slowly, Nevil released the pressure on Shauna's arm. He then took his hand and brushed a few strands of hair that had fallen across the girl's face. "Good, Shauna. I'm glad we understand each other. You may continue with the polishing."

It was only after Nevil had left the kitchen that Shauna's knees gave way and the petrified girl slumped to the floor. Quickly, she gathered the strength to resume her polishing, but Shauna could barely steady the silver candlestick gripped in her left hand.

Chapter 1 ~ August 1846 - Maguire Cottage

Tara stretched quietly as she slipped her into her skirt, blouse, and shawl. *'Tis Saturday morning,* she thought, *my favorite day of the week.* She crept out of the bedroom hoping Grandma Cassie wouldn't hear her and would sleep awhile longer. As the oldest child in the Maguire clan, Tara learned early in life the meaning of hard work. She was a big help to her family. She was usually, the first to rise, stoking the fire with peat so the house would be warm when the others awoke. This was a particular blessing to her grandmother who, at sixty-five, suffered from aching joints. After a trip to the outside lavatory and a quick wash-up at the sink, Tara put the water to boil and began the daily ritual of making porridge and tea. As she headed to the barn to milk the cow, Mrs. Mooney, she could hear the muffled sounds of Ma talking to Diane and the twins in her parents' bedroom.

The cool morning air washed over Tara with a fine mist. Its dew settled on the wee budding wildflowers that held the promise of a beautiful day. Tara lingered on the mossy path to the barn. She watched two small badgers forage in the bushes hunting for food. "You're quite busy this morning, brave badgers. Perhaps your babies are hungry and cry for some breakfast." It seemed to Tara, that the badgers reflected the struggles of the Irish. Her father's words echoed in her head. *Everyone must work the land to stay alive. The future of Ireland lies with the land.*

"Top of the mornin' to you, Mrs. Mooney," greeted Tara. "'Tis a fine and misty summer morn'." The passive brown cow looked at Tara through lazy wet eyes. A muffled sound in the corner of the barn startled Tara to attention. A small black and white dog, flecked with bits of straw, trotted up to Tara. "Bailey, you old rascal, where have you been?" The dog looked at his mistress with tail wagging. "I called you for half an hour last night to give you the scraps from our supper, but you were nowhere to be found. Out on the town again were you, laddy? Well, your loss was the pigs' fortune, because Buddy and Bonnie dined on your dinner." Bailey cocked his head and barked as if he understood every word. Tara smiled and added, "I imagine you found something to keep you happy." The dog settled at Tara's feet as the girl pulled the milking stool next to Mrs. Mooney and began filling the pail with the warm liquid. She had performed the milking so many times, the task came as easy to her as breathing, and she sang as her hands worked in rhythm to an ancient hymn.

> *I hear the songs of Ireland calling,*
> *Under the brave and tender skies.*
> *'Tis for you my tears are falling.*
> *I see you smile through misty eyes.*
>
> *The winds of change are blowing gusty,*
> *Throughout the storms of a thousand years.*
> *Our shiny staff has grown so rusty,*
> *Under the flow of our sweet tears.*

As Tara finished, a cool breeze whispered across her face. She conceived the notion that something out of the ordinary would intrude the safety of her life. Tara shuddered and shook the thought out of her head. "Enough of this fairy-dreaming, Mrs. Mooney. The hungry ones will be wanting the milk for their porridge."

When Tara entered the kitchen, she found Granny Cassie, Ma, and the little ones seated around the oak table discussing plans for the day. "There's a chill in the air, but I believe 'twill give way to a lovely fine day," Tara said. "I thought that later in the mornin' I would check in on Mrs. Curran and the children. Since the death of her husband, she has grown to despair how the family will survive. I'll be takin' her some vegetables from my garden."

"'Tis a cryin' shame her Dennis was killed movin' the logs off Squire Dellamort's wagons, sighed Cassie "Father Scanlon told me that, although Shauna will continue to work at the manor, the squire has given the rest of the family a fortnight to move off his land."

"Tenant farming can be so very cruel when the working family can no longer produce," Elsie uttered as she shook her head.

"Take a loaf of soda bread to the family," Cassie added. "I'll bake it up fresh this mornin'."

The twins implored, "Can we come with you, Tara? We want to play with Mary and Billy while you visit with their ma." Before Tara could answer, her mother spoke.

"Finish your chores and we'll see about that, boys," said Elsie. Robbie and Joseph nodded as they ate their porridge. At that moment, Michael Maguire thrust open the door to the cottage and stood staring at his family.

"Saints preserve us, Michael, what's wrong?" asked Elsie, "You look as though a ghost has walked across your very own grave."

Michael slumped into his chair at the head of the table. "We're ruined, Elsie. God help us, we're surely ruined," he croaked. "I was diggin' up some potatoes to see if they were ready for the harvest..." Michael stopped to catch his breath. His face was as pale as the whitewash paint on the cottage walls. "The potatoes are black with poison. Every potato, black mush. I took them to the hogs. Buddy and Bonnie wouldn't even look at 'em." Absently, he made the sign of the cross. "Jesus, Mary, and Joseph…we're ruined."

Chapter 2 ~ June 1847 - Dellamort Wood

Grandma Cassie sat outside the empty cottage using her small trunk as a stool. She bent over as she prayed the Rosary and stared at the moist soil beneath her shoes. A large black shawl draped her head, and she looked like a very old woman in mourning. The nine-year old twins Robbie and Joseph fiddled with sticks in the dirt. Michael slowly gathered their meager belongings into the handcart they had borrowed from Harry Powers who owned Powers Pub in the village. Elsie carried two-year-old Diane on her hip. The child was tired and fussy.

"Please, Ma, let me carry my baby sister," implored Tara. "'Tis precious little time I have left to hold her before you go." Silent tears streaked down Elsie's face as she blindly handed her daughter to Tara.

"Gather 'round," instructed Michael to his family. "Heavenly Father, bless this land which provided for our needs these many years. Protect this family as we journey to a new country. Watch and guard our cherished Tara until we are united once more. Bless our neighbors whom we leave behind that they may not know another night of hunger. Help us understand and grow from the tragic circumstances that have forced us from our dear Ireland. In the name of the Father, the Son, the Holy Ghost, and all the saints in heaven. Amen."

"Amen," the family whispered in somber echo.

Tara looked at her family. It was hard to hide the fear in her eyes. A fear, which had terrorized her for months.

When the potato crop had failed the previous summer, the family had lost their main source of food. The money from Michael's crops of barley, oats, and flax was needed to pay the mortgage on the farm. The family frantically struggled to keep ahead of their creditors. When Michael fell behind on the mortgage to Dellamort Bank, the squire quickly foreclosed and the family lost their farm.

It had all happened so fast that Tara was still numb with the reality that everything she loved was gone. Dear Mrs. Mooney, sold to buy food for winter. The hogs and chickens, long eaten. Every scrap from her garden used to feed the little ones. Even Grandma Cassie's lovely Belleck, Da's sturdy oak table, along with every other pot and scrap of furniture sold to Mr. Fox at the second-hand shop to help pay for the passage in steerage to cross the Atlantic. Tara had cried to see Grandma Cassie sell her lovely Belleek pitcher and bowl to Mr. Fox for half its worth.

Tara remembered her parents talking around the table into the wee hours of the night looking to find the best solution to the terrible troubles that plagued them and countless other families in the area.

"I cannot stay in Ireland and become a tenant farmer like so many of our friends," Michael had whispered to Elsie and Cassie in soft angry tones. "I've seen that kind of life, and I'll have none of it. 'Tis best we sell off what we have and try our luck as immigrants in the Americas. Your brother Pat was good to invite us to come and make a go of it on his farm in Prince Edward Island, Canada. He says the land is fertile and cheap, and any man with a strong back and a desire to work can make a decent living."

"I know, Michael," Elsie had sobbed. "Katie and Patrick say the island is a trove, and 'tis much like our beloved Ireland, but to leave our home, forever. I'm wracked with worry about the trip. They say 'tis a hard voyage and many have lost their lives in the sailing. What'll the voyage do to poor Cassie and the wee children?"

"I don't know, Elsie. We're in God's hands now. In truth, I'm more worried about Tara and leavin' her to pay off the rest of the money we owe to Dellamort," declared Michael. "Indentured to that devil for a year is almost more than I can bear. I've half a mind to flee in the night and take her with us."

"We'd never make it to the next town, Michael. You know the squire owns half the village and has the arm of the law in his favor. He'd have the constable hunt us down before we could get to the next county. He's hated us these many years, and that fearsome snake would love a reason to torment us further. 'Twas a clever blessing that you made the squire put pen to paper stating he would be bound by contract to give Tara passage on a sailing vessel after one year of labor. Our family *will* be united again," lamented Elsie. "I'd have stayed myself, but with the baby and all. Cassie wanted to stay but she isn't up to the work, and you must go to get us started in the new land."

Michael patted Elsie's arm, "Don't torture yourself, love. We both know 'tis the only way. The squire allowed her to keep her puppy as long as she feeds him from her daily allotment of food. At least she'll have Bailey to comfort her at night. The little dog is the joy of her life, and he'll give her the strength to endure."

Tara sighed as she pushed away the unhappy incidents, which had brought her family to this day. She struggled to stay cheerful so that her family would not worry about her. *I must be brave so they will not sense the terror that grips my heart*

Tara walked to the village with her family. A steady drizzle began to fall, which made the handcart difficult to pull. No one spoke. Every step, every movement of the little procession was like a funeral-march. The slow pace mirrored the sadness that had settled in the canyon of their souls.

They stood in front of Powers Pub beside the rented wagon that would carry them to Dundalk Bay. When it finally became clear that they could no longer halt the current of time, Tara embraced and said goodbye to Grandma Cassie. She thanked her for the hours of stories she'd told her in bed before they went to sleep each night. She kissed the twins, and they cried when she did not get on the wagon with them to go sailing on the big ocean. She handed sweet Diane, who had fallen asleep on the walk to the village, and kissed her softly on the forehead. "Be a good little lass for Ma," Tara whispered as she buried her face in her mother's waist.

Michael guided Tara a few steps away from the family. "Tara," Michael croaked, "remember to say your prayers each night, use you gardening skills to tend to your daily work with pride, and come home to us soon, lass. If you need anything, Father Scanlon said he'd look after you. Your Ma will write when we arrive at Uncle Pat and Aunt Katie's farm." He gathered Tara into his arms, thinking how small she felt. He squeezed his daughter as he squeezed his eyes shut to hold back the tears.

"I'll make you proud, Da," cried Tara into his chest—forgetting her promise to be brave. And then it was done. The wagon wheels creaked as it pulled away. Tara waved and watched her entire family leave. She watched until there was nothing left of them but the muddy tracks in the road. A sudden chill gripped her heart with an icy truth. She was twelve and alone in Ireland. The village clock chimed twice as Tara and Bailey began the walk to Dellamort Estate.

Her paltry belongings had already been brought to the tiny room that would shelter her for the next year. It was a small converted tool shed situated at the back of the finest stable Tara had ever seen. The ceiling had been hand carved in intricate designs. The high vaulted roof looked like pictures she had seen of cathedrals in books. Beautiful arched windows allowed ample light to spill into the stable. Tara could not believe that something so grand was made for the pleasure of horses that could not appreciate the beauty of it all. The walls of the stable were made of thick stone, and would keep Tara from freezing during winter.

On the walls of her cramped little shed, hung a variety of garden tools. The hoes, rakes, and shovels were for Tara's use tending the squire's garden. A wooden crate served as a table, and her mattress was nothing more than a bed of straw on a wooden box-frame. Michael had nailed it together so she would be up off the cold floor. He had also fitted a slide lock so the door could be bolted from the inside, and that gave Tara an added measure of comfort. Elsie and Granny Cassie worked nights to fill her rag quilt with extra feathers so she would stay warm.

But the best thing in the shed was the calendar that Cassie had given her. Michael had nailed it to the door with a pencil attached by a length of string. The calendar would mark the days until next July when the squire's debt would be paid, and she could sail home to her family. A narrow rectangular window, which had been cut into the wall above the door, let in a sliver of light from the stable. Tara's day would begin at five o'clock in the morning, and her alarm was the crowing of a fat rooster that lived in a nearby barn. Sunday was the Sabbath and her only day off. It was a day to go to Mass in the morning, wash her clothes and hair, and prepare for work again on Monday.

A butler, named Nevil Hawkins, had already interviewed Tara. She had also briefly met Mrs. Larkin, the cook who managed the kitchen staff. Tara thought the butler was a frightening little man. She did not like the way he glared at her with hungry eyes like she might make a savory snack. His instructions had made her shiver. "You'll work from sunrise until dark overtakes the day, and sometimes into the night if the squire's having a party. You will weed and tend the garden to the rear of the kitchen. The tools are in your shed. Lose them and you'll pay for them. You will help with the laundry, and do any other manner of things in which the servants might need assistance with. The kitchen staff will provide two meals per day, and if the dog becomes a problem," the butler paused, "I will personally drown the mutt in the wash basin near the back porch. We'll have no slackers on this estate, or you will be put out with the rubbish in the morning. Do I make myself clear?" Tara had nodded, knowing that the butler meant every threatening word.

Tara wondered if she should stick to the main road, but decided she could make faster time if she cut through Dellamort Wood. Although it was heavily guarded with keepers, many of the village people used the woods to poach pheasant from the forest, or trout from one of the squire's lakes. For the most part, Tara had always stayed out of the forest because she did not like Squire Dellamort. Tara knew that he had been after her family's farm for many years, and she made it a practice to stay away from his land. She had never spoken to him personally and doubted if he even knew what she looked like. Although she had never told anyone her feelings, Tara thought the squire was a vile, mean man.

Once, when she was nine, she had seen him kick a small puppy who was sleeping on the steps of Dellamort Bank. The squire was annoyed because he had to step over the unlucky dog who blocked his entrance to the bank. The poor creature yelped as the squire's boot laid into its haunches. It limped to the side of the bank and dropped in the dirt to lick its wound. Tara ran over and saw that the metal toe of the squire's riding boot had sliced into the hip of the poor creature. The small dog's fur was matted with blood. Tara ran over to the pub and asked Mr. Powers for a wet rag. She cleaned the wound while the scared pup shivered and whined in pain. Tara sang a soothing lullaby until the puppy fell asleep. It was clear that the scrawny dog was a stray. After some time, Tara picked it up and carried it home. She had not yet reached the cottage when she decided to name him Bailey.

Tara slipped through a hedge and found the path that cut through a meadow leading to Dellamort Wood. "'Tis our last day of freedom, Bailey, so we must try to make the best of this very sad day." She stopped for a moment in the small meadow. In the distance, two red deer grazed on some grass near a small lake. They glanced her way but continued eating. Several beautiful swans floated gracefully across the glassy water. Two black swans mingled among the white. *Look at how happy they are in each other's company*, thought Tara. *Why can't people learn the lessons that the Lord's creatures already seem to know?*

"Bailey, did you know that another name for a black swan is a mucky duck?" asked Tara. "Isn't that funny? I wonder who thought that up?" Bailey cocked his head in Tara's direction as if waiting for her to continue. Tara laughed as she spoke, "Well, I must say, laddy, you're a good student today." Bailey opened his brown eyes wider and stared at his mistress. "You stay close at hand, young man. I don't want to be losin' you in here. I shudder to think what your fate might be. Squire Dellamort's hounds might eat you for a snack!" The girl pressed on with Bailey at her heels. It was unusual for the dog to stay so close. It was as though he also sensed that they were in unwelcome territory. Gradually the clearing gave way and Tara followed a path into the dense forest.

Tara had to admit that the trees of Dellamort Wood were as lovely as those described in an enchanted fairy tale. Large majestic oaks formed a canopy over the forest sheltering it like an umbrella. An understory of smaller shade loving beeches, hemlocks and maples added texture and a woody incense smell to the natural surroundings. Cardinals and robins nestled in the branches of the trees with squirrels, pheasants, and grouse. Foxes, badgers, mice, and deer were among the many other animals that made the magnificent woodland their home.

It occurred to Tara that nothing in a forest ever stands still. *Old trees die and make room for new ones. Animals lose their struggle with life and decay into humus. The cycle of life helps the forest to thrive in glory.* The morning's drizzle had given way to a bright sunny day, and rays of sunlight poured through the branches of the trees. Streaks of light cascaded on the leaves and onto the forest floor. To Tara, it felt as though she were in a cathedral more beautiful than any built by man. *There is such a sense of reverence and harmony betwixt the plants and animals. A forest is truly one of God's finest creations.* Tara pressed on. The girl never suspected that this afternoon would be the last moment of peace she would know for sometime.

Chapter 3 ~ June 1847 - Dellamort Estate

Tara awoke early the next morning, long before the rooster crowed. The girl lay huddled in bed with her dog, reluctant to face the day ahead. She pressed her nose to the rag quilt and breathed its scent. It smelled of a peat fire from the kitchen hearth; it reminded her of home. She wondered where her family had spent the night.

Tara had not slept well in the little shed. She remembered her terrible dream about a massive giant sitting on a gigantic pillow. He sat with a crown on his head yelling for food. Many small people were cooking roasts, potatoes, pies, and hams so that they would not have to listen to the giant bellow about how hungry he was. But no matter how much they cooked, the little workers could not quench his hunger or thirst. Tara was tired and hungry just thinking about the dream, and it occurred to her that she had eaten nothing but a hunk of bread at breakfast the previous day. Bailey licked her face and that brought her back to what she needed to do today. Survive. Her family was gone and she was at the mercy of Dellamort Estate. She said a quick prayer to Saint Catherine to give her courage and one to Saint Christopher, the patron saint of travelers, to guard her family on their journey. Quickly, she stood to get dressed.

The morning was cool and damp as Tara made her way to the lavatory near the back of the stable. She had been told that she would share this privy with the kitchen help and the stable boy who took care of the squire's horses. She found a large washing basin filled with water. The icy cold water tingled as she cleaned her face, neck, hands, and arms with a small rag and a bar of soap Cassie had packed for her.

Bailey sniffed the bushes looking for a rabbit to chase. "Here, fella," Tara whispered softly. She watched him take care of his morning business and then tiptoed back to the shed. The dog followed his mistress to their room. She hung the washrag on a nail and placed the bar of soap on a wooden ledge. "Well, I guess it's time to face the day." She walked to the door of the shed. "You stay, laddy, until I come back for you." Tara closed the door and made her way to the kitchen.

Shauna Curran waved Tara into the warmth of the mansion. "My, but you're up early!" The girl spoke in rapid whispers. "'Tis so nice to have someone I know come work at the estate," Shauna said as she looked over her shoulder nervously. "I've been so lonely since Da died, and Ma went to live with her sister in Ballybay." Shauna's thick red hair was pulled up inside her crisp white mobcap. She had lovely green eyes just the shade of new spring ivy. A warm smile awarded Shauna the largest dimples Tara had ever seen. She was taller than Tara and had a little more meat on her bones. "Three of us work in the kitchen most of the time. Unless the squire is havin' one of his parties. Then I 'spect you'll be called into service. Cook's name is Mrs. Larkin, and she's okay. If you work hard and stay on her good side, she'll treat you fair." Shauna leaned in and spoke softly, "'Twould be wise to watch out for Mary Tully. She serves most of the meals to the squire and would stab you in the back if 'twill make her look good in the eyes of the butler. She might act all sweet and smiles but watch that one. I think she spies for him, so be careful what you say and do around her. 'Tis true, Mr. Hawkins scares the breath out of me. Be careful of him, Tara. I think he's a mean bully, and I don't like him." Shauna continued to speak in faint whispers while looking over her shoulder as if she expected someone to hear her. "I can't believe the squire let you keep Bailey. The butler watches the food around here like a jackal, but I'll try to save him some scraps of meat and the odd bone. 'Twould be best for us if they didn't think we know each other. Goodness lass, you look as though you cried most of the night. I'm sorry for your troubles. How long will you be working here?"

"Da took Ma, Granny Cassie, the twins, and baby Diane to the Americas yesterday. Da owed the squire money, so I have been indentured to work for him for a year. After Da's debt is paid, the squire's promised to book passage for me on a ship so I can join my family next July. 'Twas the only way. I don't mind, but I sure do miss my kin." Tara looked around the kitchen. It was spotlessly clean. Large shiny white shelves along the walls held all sort of pans, pots, pitchers and bowls. Everything was polished to a shine and stacked in neat orderly rows. A huge pantry at one end of the kitchen held sacks of flour and sugar, jars of preserved fruit, molasses, eggs, onions and smoked hams. The last time Tara had seen so much food was in Mr. Eagan's produce shop in the village. A gleaming white table inhabited the middle of the room and appeared to serve as a work-table for preparing meals and a place for the servants to eat. The size of the kitchen baffled Tara. It was bigger than her entire cottage. An enormous iron stove completely covered one wall near a sink. Tara had never seen anything like it before in her life.

"My, but you're brave!" praised Shauna. "'Tis thirteen years I am now, and I still miss Ma, Billy, and Mary so much. I haven't seen them since they moved to Ballybay after Da died last year. How old would you be now, Tara?"

"I turned twelve in April."

"You've grown these past months and look at your shiny black hair all lovely," admired Shauna. "'Tis so thick and curly. I wish' mine wasn't so flamin' red...."

At that moment Mrs. Larkin, the cook, burst in through a side door that lead down stairs into the basement of the mansion. She was a large plump woman with grayish hair, which she had tied into a bun. "What have we here? Work and talk, girls, we must always work while we talk. An idle hand is the devil's playground. Ah, you're the new girl. What's your name again, love?"

"My name's Tara Maguire, Mrs. Larkin."

"Well, I like that you're an early riser. Early bird catches the worm, I always say. Not many 'round here make it to the kitchen before meself. You may call me Cook or Mrs. Larkin. Where's Mary, Shauna? That one will try anythin' to get out of sight when work's to be done. She had better get here before Mr. Hawkins makes his way to the kitchen."

Mrs. Larkin was very efficient and busied herself putting water in a big copper kettle to boil. The enormous stove had already been stoked with wood, and Cook began frying large rashers of bacon in a huge cast iron pan. Tara thought she would faint with hunger at the smell of the savory salted pork. "Well now Tara, you'll work in the garden until nine o'clock tending to the weeds and such. Squire Dellamort will not tolerate a single weed in his garden. Remember, dear, a stitch in time saves nine, so keep after the weeds," she advised in parental tones. "The squire usually takes his breakfast at eight o'clock unless he's had a late night. The staff eats when he and any guests are finished. Wash up and come for a bit o' breakfast at nine," Mrs. Larkin said pointing to a clock on the wall. "I'll ring a bell so you'll know the time. Now, come to my kitchen clean or don't come at all. I'll not tolerate slovenly deportment. A clean body is a clean mind, I always say."

"Yes, Mrs. Larkin," whispered Tara.

"Good Lord, child, you're as thin as a post. When did you last eat?" quizzed Cook.

"I had a bit of bread and a spot of tea with my family yesterday morning, ma'am."

"Dreadful, just dreadful." Mrs. Larkin cut a thick slice of bread from a large loaf resting on the sideboard. She dipped it in the bacon drippings from the pan. "The state of affairs in this poor country is absolutely disgraceful," Cook mumbled, as if talking to herself. "Take this bread and hurry on your way. Don't think this is going to become a habit, but I can't have you faintin' in the garden."

"Thank you, Mrs. Larkin." As Tara scurried out the back door to fetch the garden tools from her room, she bumped headlong into a pretty young woman coming up the steps.

"Watch where you're going, you dolt!" snarled the young maid clothed in a long black dress and white apron. It was the same uniform worn by Shauna and Mrs. Larkin.

"I'm very sorry," pleaded Tara. "You must be Mary Tully. 'Tis pleased I am to meet you." Before she could say anything further, the unhappy girl cut Tara off with a look and pushed passed her as though she were nothing more than an annoying leaf that had blown into her face.

Tara watched her sweep into the kitchen with the air of someone who appeared to be very confident and very bored at the same time. Mary had chestnut brown hair and hazel-colored eyes. She was rather short with a thin waist and full hips and thighs. At that moment, it was difficult to tell that Mary was pretty because the scowl on her face gave her a sour look. Tara stumbled wide-eyed to the path that led to the stable.

"Look Bailey, I brought us breakfast." Tara broke the bread in half and fed it to the dog. "You can come with me when I work in the garden, but I'm locking you in here when I can't keep an eye on you. I don't want you to get into any mischief when I'm not around. 'Tis for your own good, boy." Tara devoured every crumb of the bread, but her stomach rumbled for more. She removed some gardening tools from the wall and proceeded to the garden with Bailey.

Tara pushed open the heavy garden door. A magnificent garden enclosed in ivy-covered brick walls, lay before her. The walls were taller than any Tara had ever seen. Long rows of vegetables grew in neat precision between cobblestone paths. Each variety was thoughtfully labeled with a small wooden sign, which had been carefully nailed on a stick and driven into the earth. Neatly pruned fruit trees grew along the west wall. Tall vines twisted carelessly on wooden frames and Tara recognized several varieties of beans and peas. A beautiful glass greenhouse rested on the southwest corner of the garden to take full advantage of the sun. Tara was enchanted. *Whoever tended this garden did so with love.* The garden looked as though it had been only recently neglected. Tara set to work, tilling the soil with a hoe. After a thorough search of the area, Bailey settled on the path next to her to watch her work.

At length, Tara heard the sound of Cook ringing the breakfast bell. She gathered her tools and walked to the shed with Bailey close behind. "You stay here, boy, and I'll bring you some breakfast." Tara took her washrag from its nail and made her way through the stable.

A tall lanky lad with sandy blonde hair led a beautiful black stallion through the stable doors. "Top of the mornin' to you, miss," greeted the stable-boy. He tipped his cap politely to Tara and continued on his way. She gave him a shy smile and made her way to the washbasin.

Tara entered the kitchen. Mrs. Larkin, Shauna and Mary were seated around the large white table, which had been set with bowls of porridge, bread and butter, and a steaming pot of tea. Shauna motioned for Tara to come sit next to her.

"Mr. Hawkins wants to see you in his office as soon as you've had your meal," instructed Mrs. Larkin. "Shauna will show you the way. Now, help yourself to some bread and tea. There's milk in the pitcher."

"Thank you, Mrs. Larkin," said Tara. "I was wondering ma'am. 'Tis a beautiful garden, and plain to see that 'twas tended with love. What happened to the previous gardener?"

"Not that 'tis any of your business," smirked Mary Tully, "but the old goat was consumed with the black lung, and the blood he spit up killed him a fortnight ago. For the life of me, I can't imagine why the squire would want a runt like you tendin' his garden. Looks as though you'd blow over in a stiff wind."

"I know a wee bit about plants. I expect my Da told the squire I had some knowledge about growing things," said Tara shyly.

"Really, is that so?" Mary mocked. "Well, too bad your *expert* knowledge about plants couldn't save your family's farm," she sniggered.

"That'll be quite enough, Mary," said Mrs. Larkin. "Looks to me like someone got up on the wrong side of the bed this mornin'." Cook turned to Tara. "Best eat up, child. The butler does not like to be kept waiting."

Nevil Hawkins sat writing in his ledger at a small desk, with delicately curved legs. Tara entered his small orderly office and nervously waited for him to look up. As he worked, he sipped tea from a delicate china and saucer. Tara couldn't help but notice that he held the handle of the cup with dainty petite fingers. She stood frozen, nervously waiting for the butler to take notice of her. She had the feeling that Mr. Hawkins was toying with her. At length, the small wiry butler stood and slowly made his way around the desk to address Tara with small penetrating gray eyes.

"You and your family," he began, "have been a thorn in the side of this estate for too many years to count." As the butler spoke, he circled Tara like a vulture searching for something to eat. "But all that has come to an end. Has it not, my dear?" he snarled.

"It has, sir."

"You'll take your orders from me now. Do I make myself clear?"

"You do, sir."

"Good. It's important that you understand what I'm saying," he voiced in cunning tones. "You will begin work when the sun rises, and you'll work until the day is dark. I'll be watching you, and I had better never see you resting on the job," said the butler through clenched teeth. "The squire will be compensated for the aggravation he has endured from the likes of you and your family. If you break something, extra time will be added to your debt. Have I made myself clear?"

"You have, sir."

"Are these rags the best clothes you own?"

"'Tis, sir." Tara looked down at her best skirt, blouse and shawl.

"I will instruct Cook to have a uniform made so that when you work in the kitchen you do not embarrass the squire and his guests. When you work outside you can wear these rags. You're dismissed." He waved her away and continued his work in the ledger.

As Tara turned to leave, she noticed a bowl and pitcher on a small table in the corner of the office that looked strangely familiar. Her mouth fell open and she let out a gasp. Nevil Hawkins looked up from his work. "What are you carrying on about now, you foolish child?" he yelled.

"'Tis nothing, sir," Tara managed to say, "I was just admiring the lovely porcelain pitcher and bowl on the table."

"Yes, well it's clear you have an eye for nice things," he boasted. "I bought the set last month at Fox's second-hand shop in the village for a song. It's Belleek, but I guess you wouldn't know about something as fine as Belleek. It's amazing what one can pick up these days. I have acquired several nice pieces over the past year. One person's loss is another man's gain," he said laughing.

"I'm sure 'tis true. I'll be going now, sir," she mumbled.

As Tara exited the butler's office to make her way to the kitchen Mary appeared at the door. From the agitated look on Mary's face, Tara had the feeling that the girl had been standing there for some time.

She ignored Tara, curtsied to the butler, and said sweetly, "I'll take your tea tray away if you are finished, Mr. Hawkins."

"Yes, you may clear the tray away," the butler ordered. "You know, Mary, that little maiden is going to be a real beauty when she rounds out a bit. There's something about her that I find very alluring," the butler proclaimed. Nevil knew that the comment would annoy Mary, and he loved pitting the servants against each other.

Mary knew better than to say what she really felt, but had the butler looked up he would have seen that the expression on her face was not pretty. Up until now, Mary had been able to entice the butler to get the easiest chores, and she decided then and there that she did not want competition from that little worm. In angry silence, Mary made her way to the kitchen.

Chapter 4 ~ Summer 1847 - Dellamort Estate

Throughout the long days of summer, Tara's life fell into a pattern of work and sleep. She had always known how to toil over a job, but now Tara toppled into bed at night exhausted and sore. Her backed ached from hours bent over weeding and tilling the garden. Each night, she forced herself to drag a bucket of water into the shed to scrub a body caked with dirt and grime. As hard as the work was, she liked utilizing her talents to make the squire's garden flourish. Tara experimented with various composts to keep insects and beetles away from her plants. She found that a mixture of ground onion, tansy, and tobacco sprinkled among the rows of green plants proved to be an effective compound in keeping pests at bay.

As much as Tara enjoyed applying her skills to produce the bounty of food used to feed the squire and his many guests, there was just too much work for one person. Her hands were cracked with cuts. Blisters and welts formed into calluses on her palms. Sometimes she looked up from her labors to find the butler watching her from a distance. His cold stare sent shivers through her body. When the handle of an old digging trowel broke, the butler added the expense of fixing it to her time of service. The cruel gesture only made Tara more determined to finish her year and leave the estate.

The girl, who had always been carefree and trusting by nature, took stock of her situation. She became cautious. At mealtimes, Tara politely answered questions put to her, but rarely initiated conversation. She guarded her words carefully and was not overly friendly with Shauna in the company of others. Tara came to rely more and more on Bailey for comfort and companionship. She spoke to him in soft whispers when they were alone in the garden, or when they huddled in bed at night. Although she was on good terms with the stable boy, who had introduced himself as Danny, she had little time to chat and get to know him well. Tara missed her family dearly. She was very lonely.

One day, Tara found that she could find freedom from her situation by traveling outside her daily existence in her mind. She discovered how to be in another place at another time. She learned how to recall every object in the cottage as it once was before the troubles came. She could sit at the big oak table and remember every nick and scratch on its surface. Then she would travel out the kitchen door to the path that led to the barn. The smells of Mrs. Mooney and the hay inside the barn filled her with happiness and longing. She found she could play games with the little ones and bake bread with Ma. She listened to Cassie tell her stories as they cuddled in bed on a winter's night. She would chat with Da about the land. Days became weeks, and as hard as her life had become, she was cheered each morning when she could put another X on the calendar. Each mark took her closer to her family.

Tara received two meals a day as payment for her long hours of service. The food was not plentiful but enough to keep her healthy. Shauna became her secret friend. She slipped extra bones and meat scraps into the shed for Bailey when she could. On Sundays, the girls would attend Mass together. The walk to the village left them both sad and depressed. The roads were scattered with hollow-eyed women and children begging for food. Sometimes their mouths were stained green with the grass they ate to help stave the hunger in their bellies. The grass did not sustain them and they died anyway. They died by the roadside where they lay because they could not take a step further. So many people died that large mass graves were being dug to bury the poor souls whose family could not afford a proper burial.

As Tara and Shauna walked to Saint Michael's for Sunday Mass, the girl's talked about the troubles in Ireland. "The work on the estate 'tis hard, but we're so much better off than the poor folks who have nothin' but the rags on their backs." Shauna thought of her mother and sighed.

"I don't understand how one man can have so much and so many others have nothing," whispered Tara. "There's enough food on the estate to feed the entire population of this village."

"The squire has posted more signs that trespassers will be shot if they come onto his land," added Shauna, "but, they only poach from his land because they're starvin'."

"'Twill only get worse when winter begins to close in on us. God help us all then," Tara whispered.

Father Patrick Scanlon greeted the girls outside the door after Mass. "Tara, I have wonderful news. A letter from your family came in the post for you." Father pulled the letter from inside his cassock pocket and handed it to her. "I know you'll be of a mind to write them back. When you've done so, I'll see to the mailing for you."

"Thank you Father," said Tara joyfully.

"I must go now child, and help Sister Mary Martin serve the soup for the poor and starving." The priest looked tired as he strode away.

The girls walked to the side of the chapel and sat on a bench near the entrance to a cemetery. Mounds of freshly dug earth dotted the graveyard. The unsettled landscape triggered a dream Tara recently had of giant moles burrowing in the dirt, which mysteriously turned into graves. She shuddered.

The sound of Shauna's voice pulled Tara from the thoughts of the nightmare. "You're so lucky that you can read. "How'd you learn?"

Tara looked at Shauna and smiled. "Everyone in our family can read. Even when the Penal Laws were enforced before 1829, and we Irish couldn't own land in our own country or learn to read, Granny Cassie was taught in secret at the Hedge School. Our family has always set great store in books. With Da, it has always been the land, and with Ma, it was always the readin' and the writin'. My Da named me Tara because it means earth from the Latin origin. Granny says that most people don't appreciate what they have until 'tis taken away from them."

"I know, I sometimes wish that I could've let my Da know how much I loved him. I was so young when he died. Then Ma, and Billy and Mary, had to move off the squire's land. I still miss him to this day."

Tara reached for her friend's hand. "Shauna, I'd be pleased to teach you the letters so that you can learn to read and write too, but just now I'll be wantin' to read Ma's letter once through myself, if you don't mind. Then I'll gladly share its contents with you."

Shauna nodded, and respectfully moved a few paces away. She sat down on the grass and left Tara to her letter.

With hands that shook, Tara carefully tore open the letter written in her mother's own sweet hand. She had never received a letter from anyone in her young life. To get a letter that had traveled all the way across a giant ocean filled her with awe. It was a long letter written on paper so thin she knew that it would tear if she were not careful. Thought Tara, *This is a piece of the family I love so much. I will read it everyday to* bring me closer to them. I must read it slowly now to savor the importance of this occasion.

14 August, 1847

Dearest Tara,

The voyage across the Atlantic was quite difficult for everyone. We sailed out of Newry on a small square-rigged sailing barque called Providence. Our tickets for passage were in steerage. We were supposed to receive eight pints of water a day, plus flour, salt, sugar, tea, butter and ham each week. Once we were out to sea, it was clear that the captain had not enough supplies to feed all of us. A few unhappy passengers complained, and were beaten by the first mate. They were told that the captain would have them in chains if they made more fuss. There was naught we could do, so we tried to make the best of the situation.

Despite the troubles with the food, we made good progress for the first few weeks of the voyage. We shared large cooking fires that were placed on the deck of the ship. Sometimes the cooking areas were so crowded that all we ate were hard sea biscuits that could break a tooth if we were not careful. We learned to soften them in our tea. On our twenty-fifth day at sea, a violent storm broke over us, and all the steerage passengers were ordered below deck. It was very crowded in the hold of the ship, and very dark. There were no windows and we could not light a lantern for fear of fire. Our sleeping berths were nothing more than wooden shelves stacked high against the sides of the ship. Luckily, we were able to secure four narrow beds for our family. We were crowded together like sausages in a pan. The captain had overbooked the ship, so some poor folk had to sleep on crates or trunks, and others on the floor of the ship. I don't know how they got any sleep, as there were puddles of water everywhere. For three days the wind blew, and the wood on the ship's sides groaned and creaked. At times I feared we would all go to a watery grave in that floating coffin. We all prayed night and day. Ship fever broke out and spread quickly among the passengers. Many banged on the two doors leading up to the deck to let in some air, but no one came to our aid. The children were very frightened and Cassie, Da and I took turns amusing them with stories and songs. Everyone was praying and crying out for mercy. We were all hungry, and everyone was thirsty. The horrible smell inside our hold was something I will never forget.

On the third day of the storm, Cassie came down with the fever. On that day the gale blew over, and the captain ordered the doors of the hold to be lifted open. People staggered onto the deck begging for food and water. That day, fourteen souls were quickly sewn inside some canvas bags. They were tossed over the side of the ship with nothing but a stone to take them to their watery graves. Cassie seemed to rally for a while, but she never fully got her strength back. After forty-six days at sea, we arrived at a place called Grosse Isle to be processed for admittance into Canada. So many people were sick that a temporary hospital was set up, but it had not enough beds. Many had to lie on straw on the floor.

It was at this place that our dear sweet Cassie passed on. We buried her in a grave with many other people. 'Tis a miracle that the wee little ones did not get sick. I know, darling Tara, that you are crying as you read this news, and that you will be sad for many days to come. Cassie told me, before she died, that she would watch over you in heaven, She asked me to tell you not to grieve too much for her. She had a good long life and was happy to be joining Papa Frank. I think of her everyday, and talk to her as I go about my work. How I wish I could be with you at this very moment and hold you in my arms, love. You must be strong. Cassie will help you get through this.

Finally we are settled with brother Pat and his wife Katie on a dear place called Prince Edward Island. This land reminds us so much of Ireland. Beautiful beaches surround the island. You'll never guess what we discovered. The same Irish moss washes up on shore here that we have in Ireland. We feel akin with this land that grows lovely white potatoes that are healthy and strong. Land is cheap here, and there is plenty of work for all. Your Da helps Patrick on his farm, but he thinks we can save enough money to buy some land of our own next year.

The children grow healthy and strong. You would not believe how big they are. We long for the day when we can have you here with us. We, too, are keeping a calendar. Each evening after prayers, we mark off the days until we are a family once more. Be a good girl. Work hard. I am enclosing a little money so that you can write back. 'Tis not much, but we know 'twill help some.

You are always in our thoughts and prayers.

Love, Da, Ma, Robbie, Joseph, and Diane

Tears flooded into Tara's eyes, and she could hardly see the words to finish the letter. Shauna knew that something was amiss, but had the grace to leave Tara to her own thoughts. *Granny Cassie, gone. It cannot be true. All the lovely stories she told me of her childhood. I will bury those stories in my heart like jewels in a treasure box. As long as I can remember her in my heart, she'll never be truly gone from me.*

It took Tara many more minutes to stop her heaving sobs. She did not even realize that Shauna had come to sit next to her and was holding her like Cassie used to do when she was sad. She let herself be petted for a few more minutes. Then, she read the letter once more aloud and both girls cried. They shared remembrances of Cassie and Shauna's father, Dennis, for almost an hour before Tara stood up and brushed the grass from her dress.

"Let's go to Mr. Eagan's shop and buy some paper so I can write a letter home. Then we'll light a penny candle for Granny Cassie and ask Father Scanlon to say a Mass for her."

Chapter 5 ~ Autumn and Winter
1847 - Dellamort Estate

The days grew shorter and shorter. By the end of autumn there was less to do in the garden. Gradually, more of Tara's work was spent indoors helping Cook preserve all varieties of vegetables and fruits in jars for the winter. Carrots, turnips, and onions had to be stored in the cellar along with several kinds of apples. Fresh herbs were hung from the ceiling to be dried for winter use. Tara's favorite days were when Cook sent her to the forest to pick the last of the wild berries, and to hunt for mushrooms that would also be dried and stored for winter. Mrs. Larkin was especially delighted when Tara discovered a beehive in Dellamort Wood. She sent the stable boy and Shauna to assist Tara with the harvest. Tara showed Danny and Shauna how to smoke the hive to calm the bees. The three carried the thick honeycombs back to the kitchen in enamel buckets. Cook and the girls extracted enough honey from the waxy combs to fill four quart crocks.

In October, the squire hosted a shooting party for all the notables in the area. Bloated hunters in tan breeches and black boots swarmed Dellamort Wood to shoot the pheasant the keepers had been raising over the past months. Tara and Shauna chuckled as they heard Danny describe the day.

"The darlin' birds never had a chance. The keepers had been fattenin' them up with so much cornmeal, they could barely fly up into the trees to roost at night. The birds were so used to being fed, they were almost tame. The way they carried on, you would've thought the men were hunting big game on an African safari."

At the beginning of November, the Squire left the estate to travel in Europe where the weather was warmer. He was expected back mid December to host his annual Christmas gala for forty distinguished guests.

Like a general with his army, Nevil drove the staff to exhaustion preparing the mansion for the numerous guests staying over during the weekend event. With the squire gone, even Danny was called away from some of his stable duties to carry heavy Persian carpets outside to be dusted with wooden beaters. Every square inch of space in the mansion was scrubbed, waxed, and polished. Tara shined the silver so brightly she could see her reflection as though she were looking in a mirror. Once, while cleaning the floor of the butler's office, she gently picked up Grandma Cassie's pitcher and held it against her cheek. Tears welled in her eyes as she thought, *Oh Granny, I know that this will always be a part of you, and in some strange way, it's here to remind me that you are watching over me in heaven.* Tara tenderly kissed the pitcher, carefully replaced it inside its bowl, and walked out of the room.

"I never imagined that anyone could own so many beautiful things," whispered Tara to Shauna as they polished brass spittoons in the kitchen. "Fancy all this for one man," she continued gesturing with her eyes.

"'Tis sinful if you ask me," added Shauna, "with so many dyin' of the hunger on the roadside outside the estate." Both girls quickly looked down at their work when Mary entered the kitchen carrying two more brass spittoons under her arms.

"What's all the whispering going on in here?" she questioned in a bossy tone. "There's too much work to be done, so shut your gobs before I tell Nevil what you're up to," threatened Mary.

"Oh, 'tis Nevil now is it?" questioned Shauna. "I didn't know that you were on a first name basis these days."

Realizing that she may have said too much, rattled the butler's pet servant. In a huff, Mary thrust the spittoons at Shauna and pivoted to leave the kitchen. At that moment, an unfortunate event occurred. Mary stepped directly in a small puddle of water, which had not been mopped up properly after breakfast. Her legs flew out from underneath, and she flew straight up in the air. Both girls stared in horrified amazement as Mary landed on her backside looking like a turtle upended on its shell. At that moment, Mrs. Larkin entered through the basement door in time to see a flurry of petticoats, pantaloons, and legs flailing about. She was startled to hear a gaggle of swear words stream from Mary's mouth.

"What's all the brouhaha goin' on in here?" Cook demanded. "And you, with the mouth of a guttersnipe. If you can scream that loud, you can't be very hurt."

Rubbing her bottom, Mary rose to face Mrs. Larkin. "'Tis just that I slipped in this wet spot..."

"And why, might I be askin', is there a wet spot on the floor?" inquired Cook as she faced all three girls with a look that would freeze flames. "Well now, let's not hem and haw!"

The silence of a funeral parlor hung in the air until Mary mumbled sheepishly, "I guess I missed this spot when I mopped the floor earlier, Mrs. Larkin."

"Then, you've none to blame but yourself, so stop looking so down in the mouth. A job isn't worth doin' unless 'tis done right, I always say. Now, enough of this dallying about. There's work to do and by hook or by crook, it will be done."

Mary limped out of the kitchen rubbing her bottom with her hands. Tara and Shauna listened as Mrs. Larkin made her way to another part of the house mumbling something about "not suffering fools gladly."

Several minutes of quiet passed before Shauna whispered, "Pride goeth before the fall, I always say," in her best imitation of Mrs. Larkin.

A kernel of laughter welled inside Tara's chest. She tried to hold it in, but the urge to giggle was more than she could bear. Her shoulders heaved and her body shook with muffled sounds of laughter. Shauna, also, was having a hard time containing herself. Both girls held their stomachs and laughed in silent glee until tears streamed down their faces. Eventually they got composed enough to attend to the polishing, but all morning they chuckled over and over when they thought of the spectacle Mary had made of herself.

Later, as they were beating the dust from some carpets outside the kitchen door, Tara confessed, "Shauna, 'tis the first time that I have laughed in over a year. 'Tis powerful good medicine for the body to be laughin'. I'll never forget the sight of those legs flappin' about in the air like a dying beetle on its back." The girls used the sound of their sticks to muffle the laughter that erupted once again.

The squire was back from France, and the staff worked day and night to prepare the feast for the grand Christmas gala. Crown roasts of beef with Yorkshire pudding, lamb seasoned with rosemary and garlic, and pheasants stuffed with apples, wild rice, and red peppercorns were roasted in the huge kitchen oven. Glazed carrots and onions piled atop baby brussels sprouts and wild mushrooms accompanied the main dishes. An enormous English trifle followed by a compote of quince and Stilton cheese rounded out the fare for the squire's guests. The display of food was staggering to Tara, and far beyond anything she had ever witnessed.

A giant evergreen tree had been cut down from the Dellamort Wood. It was set up in the ballroom and decorated with imported glass ornaments, gilded walnuts, fruits, and holly berries. Small candles, wired to the lower branches, would be lighted on the evening of the gala. Tara stared at it in wide-eyed wonderment. The piney smell of the tree delighted her senses. It was as though the forest had been brought to her. She felt she never could have imagined anything so preposterous in all her young life. The squire stood before the beautifully decorated Christmas tree like a child with a new pony and addressed his staff. Tara felt very grownup in her black dress, white apron, and crisp white mobcap as she faced the squire with the rest of the staff. As the man spoke, she became mesmerized by the different colors of his eyes.

"Queen Victoria's husband, Prince Albert, brought the custom of the Christmas tree to England from his native country of Germany. It's quite the trend in England. We may be isolated on this backward island, but we must do our best to keep up with the latest fashions of the Royal House of Saxe-Coburg and Gotha. I think my guests will be completely enchanted when they see it lighted at the ball," he said in a tone that expressed how pleased he was with himself.

Tara had also gazed in awe at the squire's display of Christmas cards over the fireplace mantle in his parlor that morning. Only the wealthy gentry in Great Britain and other parts of Europe practiced the recent custom of exchanging cards. The lithographed pictures of winter scenes had been hand colored. Some were printed with the words: Merry

Christmas and Happy New Year. Tara thought they were beautiful.

"I wish to commend your fine efforts in preparing Dellamort Manor for my gala. You will be working very hard over the next few days. I want this weekend to be the talk of the county. Do I make myself clear? Do not embarrass me! If your work satisfies me, I will declare a holiday next weekend, and grant you both Saturday and Sunday off as reward for your many hours of work these past weeks."

"On behalf of the staff," announced Nevil in a grand manner, "I wish to thank you, Squire, for this gracious gesture." Nevil clapped his hands. "All right everyone back to work. There is still much to be done."

Tara was elated as she walked to the kitchen. *Two whole days off! I will rest in bed for an extra hour before getting up, and I'll walk with Bailey in the woods. I'll write to Da and Ma and the dear little ones and tell them of the wondrous Christmas tree.*

Guests planning to stay overnight arrived early on the afternoon of the party. Nevil and Mary showed them to their rooms. Many of the ladies brought their own handmaidens with them to see to their hair and dresses for the evening's festivities. As Mary and Nevil attended to the needs of the guests, Shauna, Tara, and Mrs. Larkin put the finishing touches on the silver trays of nibbles which would be served before dinner. "'Tis the calm before the storm," lamented Cook. Nevil had coached the girls for weeks in the proper way to serve and clear away plates from the guests. Tara was very nervous.

"Line up, girls, for final inspection," barked the butler. "Shauna, your shoes are scuffed; see to it before the party. Tuck those strands of hair into your cap, Mary." Nevil circled Tara studying her for any infractions. "I must admit, our little Tara is growing into quite the young lady and a far improvement from the scrawny waft who came to work here six months ago. You're a good little worker, I'll say that for you."

Tara knew that she was expected to be pleased with the praise the butler was lavishing on her, but instead she felt embarrassed that he was drawing attention to her. She did not like the way he looked at her now. "Thank you, sir," she mumbled in a whisper. As she turned to avoid Nevil's unwelcome gaze, she noticed that Mary had a scowl frozen on her face.

Two hours later, Tara was trying to steady a silver tray as she walked among the guests serving curried kidney tarts, stuffed quail eggs, small dried figs stuffed with walnuts glazed in honey. The people spoke over her as though she were nothing more than a potted plant.

"What is the word in England on the fate of the Irish, Mr. Slaughter?" asked an elegant lady dressed in a blue silk gown and diamond necklace. The dress stood out so far from her hips, Tara couldn't imagine what manner of petticoat kept it suspended away from her legs.

"I read in *The Times* newspaper, Miss Lacey, that the British Parliament recently appointed a committee to investigate the extensive death toll, as well as the migration of the Irish out of Ireland due to the blight of the potato. The news article also reported that Francis Spaight, a British magistrate and Limerick merchant, testified before parliament that he was happy to transport his own tenants out of Ireland because he considers them to be 'dead weight.' He further testified that it would be an improvement on the land, and he considers the failure of the potato crop to be the greatest possible value in helping with the Irish emigration system," voiced Mr. Slaughter in arrogant tones as he plucked a fig from Tara's tray and stuffed it in his mouth.

"That is shocking news, Mr. Slaughter!"

"All I know," Mr. Slaughter added in a pleased tone, "is that my export company in Dublin has never been better. Last week we shipped huge cargoes of butter, oats, eggs, beef, ham, and linen to the markets in England."

"So what you're saying, Mr. Slaughter, is that there is ample food in this country, but not for the people who live here."

"It's more complicated than that, my dear, and I doubt that you would understand." Mr. Slaughter responded, hoping to quiet her criticism.

"Well personally, I think the starvation of these people is shocking," commented Miss Lacey.

"Starvation?" Mr. Slaughter questioned. "Don't you mean famine, my dear?"

"How can you call it a famine, Mr. Slaughter, when so much food is being shipped out of the country?" asked Miss Lacey in a distressed tone.

"Well now, ahem…with all due respect, Miss Lacey, delicate women, like yourself, shouldn't concern themselves in these matters…"

Tara moved away from the couple so she would not have to listen to the troubles surrounding her people anymore.

The Christmas gala was a great success for the squire. All weekend, he walked around his mansion like a peacock with its feathers puffed out, never noticing that Tara and the other servants averaged four to five hours of sleep each night. Long after the last guest headed home, the servants were still cleaning crystal and china in the kitchen. It took another four days to put the guestrooms back in order. By the time the next weekend came, Cook, Nevil, and all the household staff were tired beyond belief.

Shauna and Tara had whispered in secret tones about the enormous amounts of food served at each meal and the waste of it left on the plates. Tara had never seen anything like it in her life. In her family, food was never squandered. "The leftovers from these meals would feed half the people of Cootehill," she remarked to Shauna when they were alone in the kitchen. The girls managed to slip loads of scraps to Bailey in the shed as they took the garbage outside. The rest was taken away to feed the hogs and chickens. Tara wished she could bring some of it to the edge of the estate to feed the hungry, but she knew how heavily guarded it was. She could not risk the anger of the butler. It seemed as though he was looking for her to slip-up, and she was determined to leave in July as had been promised by the squire.

When the work was finally completed on Friday night, Tara fell into bed holding Bailey. She slept until eight o'clock the following morning. She might have slept longer if Bailey had not licked her face, which forced her up. She did all the things she had told Shauna she would do. She walked in the woods with Bailey, and after, wrote to her family. "Bailey, the family will not believe the beautiful forest tree that was lit aglow with candles. They'll think I'm fairy-talking for sure. I'll ask Father Scanlon to post my letter after Mass on Sunday." Tara knew that the priest was very distressed. Men, women, and children continued to die at an alarming rate despite his efforts with the soup. The girls did not have the heart to tell him about the enormous quantities of food at the squire's party.

Chapter 6 ~ Spring 1848 - Dellamort Estate

The days lengthened and Tara resumed her work in the garden. She was happy to be outside once more and spend more time with her little dog. When the ground softened, she moved the vegetables, she had planted in small trays in the greenhouse, to the garden. Carefully, she planted and labeled each variety as she had seen the previous gardener do. The squire had brought some potato tubers back with him from Europe, and she planted these in the hope that they would be healthy. So few potatoes had survived the mysterious blight, that there were not enough healthy tubers to replant and form into new crops. Tara received permission from the butler to revitalize the garden with soil from the forest and manure from the large herds of cattle that grazed on the eastern portion of the estate. Daily, she made trips to Dellamort Wood to gather the rich humus that rested on the forest floor into large burlap sacks to mix into the garden soil. Danny brought one of the wagons from the estate and helped her with the work. They gathered cow patties from the pastures, which Tara would blend with the humus to form the mulch.

"How come you know so much about gardenin'?" Danny asked as they were loading the sacks onto the wagon.

"I always had a garden when we lived on our farm. Da gave me a book on botany, and I read about plants and herbs. I've always had the knack to make things grow. The one thing I couldn't do was save Da from losing his farm when the potato crop failed," Tara grieved.

"My folk were tenant farmers, and they lost everything when the potatoes rotted. Last April, they took the wee ones and sailed to New York. I've not heard a word from them since they left," Danny added sadly.

"Why didn't you go with them?" asked Tara.

Danny was quiet for a few seconds, as if deciding whether he wanted to answer Tara's question. He looked at Tara and she could see that his face was slightly flushed. "'Tis sweet I am on Shauna. Though, she don't be knowin' anythin'' about it. I just decided that I had a decent day's wages, and if I stayed, there might come a chance that she'd be noticin' that I'm more than just the boy who works in the stable."

"How old are you Danny?" Tara asked.

"'Tis seventeen I'll be next month in April."

"Well saints preserve us, we share the same birthday month," Tara remarked, "I shall be thirteen-years-old on the eighteenth day of that very month my own self." Tara reflected for a few moments before she spoke again, "You know, Danny, I'm not yet a woman, yet I feel as though I left my childhood somewhere on our farm the day Da walked through the kitchen door and told us the potato crop had failed. From that moment until now, it seems that all any of us Irish have been doing is trying to survive. 'Tis glad I am that my service on this estate will finally be coming to an end on the tenth day of July. That's when the squire has promised to pay my way aboard a sailing ship, and I'll be joining my family in Prince Edward Island, Canada." Tara looked up at the tall lanky stable boy and smiled.

"Danny, if you give me the name of the ship that your family sailed on to America, I'll write to the proper authorities and try and find out the whereabouts of your kin."

"That would be grand, Tara. I'm sure there must be a ship's record of when it landed in New York. At least I'll be knowin' if they made it that far. Neither Ma nor Da can write, but they said that they'd be askin' the parish priest to be writin' a short note to me. 'Tis just a little worried I am because of the waitin' and all." Danny told Tara that a ship, called *Hannah*, sailed to New York from Liverpool, England on the third day of April last year.

At Mass on Sunday, Tara asked Father Scanlon for help. Father told her that a report of the movement of all ships around the world was kept at Lloyd's of London. "They're bound to have records of the fate of any ship," he said, "and you should start your inquiries there." Tara wrote the letter that evening.

April came and Tara drew a small star on the calendar next to the **X** marking the eighteenth day of the month. She had turned thirteen on that day. Other than Danny, she had told no one about it. It was just another day of work pulling weeds in the garden.

It took two months to get a reply, but Father Scanlon finally presented Tara with an official looking letter at Mass the last week in May. "Here are a few more books for you to borrow, girls," encouraged Father. "'Tis a grand thing that Tara is teaching you the reading, Shauna. I keep hearing wonderful reports on your progress."

"Thank you, Father," beamed Shauna.

Shauna and Tara walked to the stable directly after Mass and found Danny and Bailey napping on a large mound of fresh hay. Rays of sunlight streamed through the beautiful arched windows. Together, they made a contented picture.

"Ah, 'tis a shame to wake him." remarked Shauna, "He looks like an angel sleeping on a cloud."

At that moment Bailey popped his head up and scrambled off the hay to greet his mistress. Tara looked over at Shauna, and thought she detected a sparkle in her eyes when she looked at Danny. Inwardly, she smiled as she petted her dog. Shauna woke Danny, and the three sat on the straw.

"It's the letter, Danny, are you ready?" Danny nodded his head and Tara read him the contents of the letter.

> **From: Robert Evans-Pickering**
> **Of: Lloyd's of London**
> **To: Daniel Kelly**
> **April 28, 1848**

> *This is a report of the total wreck of the 175-ton brig, Hannah, that sailed on the 3rd of April 1847 with 12 seamen under the command of Mr. Shaw, the master. The passengers consisted chiefly of agricultural labourers and their wives and children. The passage, up to the 27th of April, was favourable. The vessel then encountered heavy winds and a quantity of floating ice. On the morning of the 29th of April, the unfortunate ship struck a reef of ice at four o'clock.*

> *The captain, and the first and second mates abandoned their passengers, seized a lifeboat, and made their escape. Forty minutes elapsed before the ship sank, allowing many passengers and crew to clamber onto the ice. Men, women, and children, clad only in night attire, were scrambling over the mass of ice. Many slipped and met with a watery grave. The last to leave the ship were some of the remaining crew who contrived to save a small*

portion of spirits and a few blankets. The seamen humanely gave up their clothing to the women, some of whom had been shockingly wounded and bruised. They were exposed to the weather for fifteen hours, when a vessel hove in sight and came to their rescue.

Captain Marshall, of the barque, Nicaragua, made a heroic attempt to rescue the 129 frostbitten passengers, and seamen. Captain Marshall reported that nearly 60 passengers perished by being crushed to death between the ice, or froze to death from the extreme weather conditions. All 129 passengers were transferred to various ships and safely transported to New York after the daring rescue initiated by Captain Marshall.

It has been ascertained that the master and the part of the crew who left the floundering emigrant ship Hannah were found four days later and were taken on to Quebec. We are calling for the deserters to be officially charged for dereliction of duty.

It is with regret that I must inform you, that none of your family was listed among the surviving passengers.

Sincerely,
Robert Evans-Pickering, Esquire

Tara finally finished reading the letter. She had to stop several times to compose herself. By the time she was done, tears were running down the faces of all three young people. Quietly, Shauna walked over and sat next to Danny on the hay. She gathered him in her arms and held him like he was a baby. Quiet sobs caused his chest to heave like swells upon the sea. No one spoke for a long time.

"I'm so sorry for your troubles, Danny. I'm sorry that in the findin', the news that came was so very bad," Tara added sadly.

"'Tis not your fault lass, and I truly appreciate the effort you made to find out the truth. 'Tis better to be knowin' now, than to hope that a letter would be comin' in the mail. I sort of thought that maybe somethin' was amiss when they didn't get a priest in New York to write Father Scanlon. It had been too long in the leavin'," bemoaned the lad. "At least they're all together. I hope they didn't suffer. I want that captain to pay for his cowardly deeds!" he cried out angrily.

The three young friends spent most of the afternoon sharing stories of the families they had lost through death or separation. Tara told them of the troubles with the farm, how her beloved Grandma Cassie had to sell her lovely Belleek, and how shocked she had been to see it on a table in the butler's office. She cried again when she told them of Cassie's death from ship fever.

Tara listened as the others each shared their own sorrowful tales. "When Da was crushed to death by the logs from the squire's wagon," sobbed Shauna, "I had no time to grieve. Ma was evicted from our home. She moved to Ballybay, and I had to stay here to work. I have no money to speak of, because I send most of it to Ma, Billy, and Mary. In truth, I never had a moment of fun until you came to work at the estate, Tara."

Some of the stories they shared were happy memories of better times. They laughed together and cried together, but at the end of the afternoon each felt better in the telling. A bond formed among the three friends that day, as strong as the bonds they had shared with their families. And finally, they were no longer alone.

Chapter 7 ~ June 1848 - Dellamort Estate

With each passing day Tara's heart began to bloom with happiness, much like the roses she was tending in the planter that bordered the squire's mansion overlooking the southern portion of his estate. The mulch she and Danny had gathered had been a grand success in the garden. The tomatoes, strawberries, and cabbages were strong and healthy. Even the potatoes that the squire had brought from Europe looked hearty. Cook had been singing Tara's praises to the butler for several weeks now, telling him she was "smart as a whip."

It was a lovely day. Shauna and Mary had opened most of the windows to air out the rooms after the long winter months. Bailey had just returned with Danny to the stable after fetching the horses from the north paddock. Tara folded the mulch into the soil around the roses, which grew in front of the squire's morning room. She added a portion of soot to the mixture, from Cook's kitchen stove, to discourage slugs and caterpillars.

Tara didn't mean to eavesdrop on Squire Dellamort and the butler. In fact, she wasn't even paying attention to their conversation until she heard the sound of her name. Tara caught her breath as the conversation unfolded.

"Nevil, I had a note from that Maguire child reminding me that her year of service will be completed on the tenth day of July. I suppose we must see to the fare for her passage in steerage to join her family in the Americas. I hate to lose that one. She's been an excellent worker, and her service has far exceeded payment on the note of debt I have held at the bank this past year. I have no choice, however. Her father made me put it in writing that I would send her packing when she completed her service. Michael Maguire was a thorn in my side even until the end," he grumbled. "His land, however, has been a bounty for this estate. Prime bit of property those five acres, and I took them for a song. Tara froze in silent outrage as she heard the squire speak of her father, and the land that he had loved so dearly. It annoyed her that he spoke of her like she was nothing but a morsel of property, and not a person with feelings.

"I agree, sir," added Nevil. "Cook has been cheering her successes in the garden and says the bounty of produce is the most abundant reservoir ever produced on the estate. I could suggest offering her wages to remain, but I don't think she would stay for any price. If you'll permit me to say, sir. I do, however, have another plan that could keep her in servitude," he voiced in cunning tones, "and it wouldn't cost you a 'brass farthing' out of pocket." Nevil laughed at himself.

The squire looked up from his newspaper with interest. He loved to conspire over a clever plan. "Go on, what little scheme have you come up with this time, Nevil?"

"If the child were to have, let us say...stolen something from the estate, some bit of silver or such. And if another servant...such as Mary, were to verify that she saw the girl take this valuable bit of property, then we would be within our legal rights to call the constable to lock her up for stealing. You then, sir, might suggest to the authorities that because of the girl's young age, you might be willing to retain the girl in service for a further couple of years...to repay her debt to society."

"Yes, Hawkins, and it would make me appear lenient in the eyes of the village. It's a brilliant plan, and we would possess her services, without any cost to me, for years to come. I like the way you think, Nevil," sniggered the squire. And when Maguire writes wondering where his daughter is, I will enjoy relaying to him that she's a thief. I shall tell him that I saved her from being shipped to Australia on a convict ship, and through my compassionate and merciful nature, I have allowed her to serve her prison time by working for me on my estate." The squire laughed with a smirk. "Nevil, you think with the cunning of a wizard."

"Indeed, it *is* a splendid plan, Squire, and virtually foolproof."

"What about Mary Tully?" asked the squire. "Are you certain that she'll go along with our little scheme?"

"To begin with, sir, Mary will do as I tell her. Besides, she happens to be very jealous of our little Tara, and has made no bones of her hatred of the girl to me. Mary has the ethics of a villain and will enjoy this charade as much as us. I know that Mary thinks she has a fair bit of competition with our little black-haired beauty. I must admit, she grows lovelier with each passing day. I, myself, shall enjoy watching her bloom into womanhood."

"What...whatever," grumbled Chase with an impatient tone of voice. "Take care of it before tomorrow night, and remember, keep my name out of it when you talk to Mary. Am I clear?"

"Quite. I understand your position completely, sir," drawled the butler. "Consider it done."

"I'd like to go riding this afternoon after tea," added the squire. "Two more tenants are unable to pay the rents on their land. I'll give them notice to vacate the estate in a fortnight. I don't care that they must go. I want the land for grazing cattle anyway. It seems easier to make a profit from cattle these days. Tonight, I'll take a quiet supper in my sitting room at eight o'clock. I'm completely knackered from playing poker last evening until four o'clock in the morning. It took me that much time to win three hundred quid from Lord Higgins. I plied him with brandy, and that made the old goat careless in his wagers," the squire said in a gloating voice.

For the past year, Tara had learned to rely on her intelligence to keep her safe, and this attitude kept her from immediate hysteria. Her head was throbbing and her heart pounded as she gathered up all evidence that she had been gardening in that spot. *When Ma said you would watch over me from heaven, Granny, she did not lie. Thank you for putting me under this window at this time. God help me, Granny, what am I to do? I must talk to Danny.*

Tara found Danny and Bailey in the stable grooming the squire's black stallion, Rogue. The moment he looked at her, he knew something was terribly wrong. "Danny, find Shauna and make an excuse to get her outside," said Tara in a voice that shook with fear. "The butler and Mary will be serving tea to the squire shortly. You must meet me in the shed. Something awful has happened and I don't have much time."

"I'll find a way to get her away from Mrs. Larkin. I'll tell Cook that I need help moving something in the stable. Where are you going?" asked Danny. His face had begun to turn the color of gray ash.

"I'm going to work in the garden. Nothin' must appear different. My life depends on it. When you get Shauna away from Mrs. Larkin, walk her through the stable doors and into my room. I'll listen for the sounds of your voices, so talk loud and I will slip away to meet you."

Thirty minutes later the three friends whispered softly inside the cramped quarters of the shed. Tara quickly told them of the plan the butler and the squire had hatched to connect Tara to the theft of some silver, and how they were going to enlist the help of Mary to confirm that she was witness to the crime. "There is naught that I can do but try to make a run for it," Tara cried.

"Go to Father Scanlon. Tell him what they're up to. He'll believe you," implored Shauna.

"I have no doubt that he'll know that I am tellin' the truth, but with Mary as an eye witness, I think there is little he'll be able to do on my behalf. The only chance for me is to try and get as far away from this place as I can."

"'Twould be madness to think that you could get on a ship to North America, lass. You've no money to speak of and no contacts to help you," said Danny.

"I shall put my trust in my faith, and know Granny Cassie will help see me to my family. I'll have no chance if I stay here one night further," announced Tara.

"When Saint Patrick was a slave in Ireland, a voice spoke to him in a dream and told him to find his way home to England across the Irish Sea. He walked over two hundred miles east to the sea in broad view of everyone. No one stopped him, even though he wore the clothes of a slave. It was as though he was as invisible as a wee leprechaun. I'll put my trust in St. Patrick that he'll guide me home to my family. I'll be leavin' in an hour," stated Tara," and I will never look back on this place, and the unfair treatment I received at its hand." Tara turned and threw her meager belongings into a cloth satchel. When she finished, she picked up Bailey and held him close to her for strength. The dog sensed that she was troubled, and he licked her neck.

Shauna shed silent tears listening to Tara tell her story, but calmed her emotions knowing that she might ruin it for her friend if she did not. "I'll gather a few food items from the kitchen for you and Bailey the moment Cook leaves the kitchen."

"Mrs. Larkin has been fair with me, Shauna. Please tell her that I took nothing from the squire. It will be up to her to believe what she wants."

"I have a little money, and I'll get it for you now," said Danny. "'Tis not much, but 'twill help some."

"I too, have a wee bit of money that I was saving to take a trip to see Ma in Ballybay," added Shauna. "I'll bring it with the food."

"I can't take your money," Tara objected. "You have needs of your own."

"We want you to have it. When you get to your family and have gotten on your feet, you can send it back to us through Father Scanlon," implored Danny.

"Let us do this wee thing for you, Tara," added Shauna. "'Twill help us believe that we were a part of something right and good. Besides, 'tis not even enough to pay for your passage, but it may be enough to get you out of County Cavan."

"Thank you, thank you both." Tara sighed gratefully. The three companions embraced, knowing that it might be the last time they would be together for a long time. A moment later, they all returned to work.

At length, Tara heard the squire riding Rogue out of the stable to survey his land. When called to supper, she was so nervous she could hardly eat any of the stew that Mrs. Larkin had prepared for the staff.

"Mrs. Larkin," said Nevil. "Squire Dellamort expressed a desire to take a light supper in his sitting room after he has finished riding. As it is nearly the close of the afternoon and no formal dinner is being served, the rest of you may finish your duties and retire for the day. Mary, I need you to clear away a few things in my office. Come with me straight away," Nevil commanded.

Cook announced that she would rest for a few minutes in her room. Mary and the butler headed for his office and the girls secretly made their way to the stable where Danny was waiting for them.

"I must go now to make use of the time I have left from this day. I will walk through the night and try to put as much distance between me and this estate as I can," uttered Tara. "With luck, they won't know that I'm missing until tomorrow. If the butler asks you where I might've gone, tell him the only person who has been a friend to me is Father Scanlon. That might send him in the wrong direction for a while. Thank you both for all you've done for me. I'll write to you, Shauna, through Father Scanlon, as soon as I can." Tara turned and took Danny's hand in hers. She then placed his hand in that of Shauna's. "Take care of her for me, Danny." Danny nodded, but he was too overcome with emotion to speak. Tara picked up her dog and her satchel, and slipped out the door with tears streaming down her cheeks. She did not look back.

Tara carried Bailey in her arms until they were a mile from the mansion. It had been raining, on and off, most of the day, but now a steady drizzle soaked through Tara's clothes. *The rain may be inconvenient, but 'twill keep most people off the road and indoors.* She stayed off the main road until she got to Dellamort Wood, but did not see a soul. She put Bailey on the ground, but he could not wander far. Danny had made a rope leash for the dog in case she needed to grab him up in a hurry and make a run for it. Tara wanted to give Bailey a chance to get the feel of the tether. She knew he wouldn't like it. "I know 'tis hard on you boy, but you'll have to trust me that 'tis for your own good," Tara coaxed in soothing tones as Bailey tried to pull away from her lead. Her plan was to take the main road to Dundalk Bay then head south to Dublin.

I'll hide during the day, and proceed at night when there'll be fewer travelers on the road. Shauna has packed us enough food to last for about three days, if we're careful. The flagon Danny gave me will come in handy. I can fill it with water from streams. The money will help us buy more food when we run out. I know it'll be important to stay out of sight. There are many robbers who would love to steal from a young defenseless girl. Tara's mind was racing with the enormous task before her.

Lost in her thoughts, Tara did not hear the sound of the horse's hooves until it was too late. Speeding around a bend in the path blazed Squire Chase Dellamort on his horse Rogue. The squire had finished the afternoon survey of his land by evicting two tenant farmers. He liked to stretch Rogue's legs before heading back to the stable. The stallion could gallop as fast as a gale wind in a storm. Tara stood frozen in panic as the horse charged into her at full speed. The steed might have killed her outright, but luck prevailed and it only sideswiped her where she stood frozen with fear. The force from the blow knocked her sideways. She was already unconscious when her head hit a sharp rock as she collapsed to the ground. The dog was luckier and as Tara stood frozen in fear, she released the rope tethered to him. Bailey shifted out of harm's way a split second before the collision.

The squire's first thought was to continue on his way, but the unexpected crash caused his horse to rear up. Rogue was shaken, and he reined the horse to a stop to calm it down. "Easy, Rogue," soothed the rider, "Settle down boy, we'll soon be on our way." Chase dismounted and led his horse to the girl crumpled by the side of the path. The small dog barked frantically over her still form. The little dog annoyed Chase. "Get out of my way," he screamed. He tried to kick the dog, but something about this man had made the dog wary, and Bailey jumped out of the way just as a boot launched at his head. Chase bent over for a closer look and recognized the girl as Michael Maguire's daughter. She lay in a pool of blood and looked dead. Blood continued to flow and seep into the wet earth.

The squire looked over his shoulder to see if anyone else was in the area. All was quiet and still, except for the incessant barking of the mutt, just out of his reach. He bent over Tara and felt her neck for a pulse. A faint rhythm beat against the back of his hand. *She looks to be in a bad way*, he thought, *and will probably be dead before I could bring help to her anyway.* It was at that moment that Dellamort hatched a cruel and cold-blooded plan.

Dropping the reins of his horse, he bent over his servant and dragged her off the path. He pulled her still body about ten yards into a wooded shrub area. The squire found a leafy branch, and swept the trail he had made so that the area looked undisturbed. He traced his steps back to the road. Blood stained the area where she had fallen. It took some time to sweep enough dirt and mud over the spot to cover all traces of the blunder.

The dog had calmed down somewhat, and was making its way to the spot where the girl lay. But the squire had ceased to care about the mutt. He was wet and cold. All he wanted was to get out of the infernal rain and have a hot bath. Chase Dellamort mounted the stallion and calmly rode in the direction of his mansion. He felt certain that the girl would not live through the night. *I'll send a search party out for her in the morning. It will look as though she came to some unfortunate end as she was trying to run away. When they bring her back to the estate Nevil can plant the silver in her satchel, and that will be that. I will enjoy informing Maguire that his daughter was a criminal. It's a pity it had to end like this. My garden never looked better*, he reflected coldheartedly.

Chapter 8 ~ June 1848 - The Tinker Encampment

A small band of Gypsies, known as Tinkers to the Irish, set up camp in a clearing by a stream near Dellamort Wood. They had arrived in the area that day, and had spent a fair bit of time searching for a suitable place to accommodate three caravans, seven horses, two dogs, and the eleven men, women, and children that formed their troupe. Migrant in nature, they traveled to various villages throughout the island. They made their livelihood by providing services to the local population. They lived by their wits and were extremely versatile. The Tinkers could mend pots and pans, repair metal tools, fix furniture, and sharpen blades. They entertained the villagers by singing, dancing, juggling, and performing acrobatic tricks much like circus performers. They told fortunes, sold elixirs, and performed minor medical procedures.

The leader of this particular band was a woman who possessed the gift of second-sight. Her name was Diviña. Diviña was noted for her abilities to see into the future. She made interpretive observations of people by examining tea-leaves, studying the palms of hands, and reading tarot cards. Diviña knew a lot about potions and herbs and served as a traveling doctor, of sorts, for those who could not afford the services of the local doctor. She was a noted mid-wife and had brought more children into the world than she could remember. She had passed this job to the two younger women who were a part of her band. If there was a problem with the birthing, her expertise and knowledge of herbal medicines was utilized.

Diviña was five when she first discovered that she had the gift of second-sight. Her mother and grandmother were noted fortune-tellers of their day. Diviña had several older brothers and sisters, but none had been blessed with the mysteries of second-sight. Her mother had despaired that she would not be able to pass on her unique talents until Diviña was born.

Five-year-old Diviña, her mother, and three sisters had been shopping in a nearby village. On the trip back to their camp, Diviña asked her mother, "Mama, why are my dolls burning?"

Distracted and deep in conversation with Diviña's older sisters, her mother replied, "Don't be silly child. You didn't even bring your dolls with you today."

When the group reached the camp ten minutes later, they found their caravan consumed in flames. The women joined other members of the troupe to form a bucket brigade and were able to save the basic structure of the caravan. As predicted, the child's dolls had been destroyed in the fire. Diviña's mother spoke quietly to her daughter while bedding her down for the night.

"I'm sorry about the caravan, Mama," expressed Diviña sadly.

"We cannot change the destiny of what is written in the stars, Diviña," said the older woman. "No one was hurt, and what was lost can be replaced. They were just things, my child. Things are not important and what we need, in time, will be returned to us."

"I miss my dolls, Mama," Diviña cried.

"Diviña, the dolls were a gift to you, but you have been given a greater gift. It is a precious gift from God, and you must use it with reverence. The dolls can be replaced, but it is important not to grieve too much for material things in this world. Those who are infatuated with wealth and power are out of spiritual harmony with the stars. There is no balance, no *kintala*, in their lives. You must remember this, child. People are important, the gifts of nature are important, but never things." Diviña listened and remembered all that her mother told her that night. It marked the beginning of the child's training to enrich and refine the mystical gift with which she had been blessed.

The Irish, who are superstitious by nature, believe in fairies, banshees, and leprechauns. These beliefs entangle the stories, ballads, and poetry of their daily lives. Any fortune-teller, worth her salt, made a decent living even in the worst of times. The gifts possessed by Diviña were sought after by many as word spread about the woman who could foretell the future. She made a good living at her trade but never charged more that she thought her clients could pay. Often, she revealed what she glimpsed for free if she thought it would help those in need find their way.

Her kind face bore the lines and creases that come to those who have lived a long time. No one knew her age, and in truth, it was difficult to discern what it might be. Diviña knew that her ancestors had migrated into Western Europe from the Balkans to escape enslavement. She had been told that her great-great grandmother had come by boat to Ireland in the early 1700s. Once there, she had found others with similar ways. Her ancestors intermarried with the native population. Many became sedentary, but others continued in the migratory ways of Gypsy life. Family bonds were strong. The Tinkers drew together for protection and to escape those who discriminated against them. They had a keen zest for life and reveled in story, music, dance, and song.

The most captivating feature about Diviña was her dark bronze eyes. When she smiled, the deep penetrating color was like a passageway to the interior of her soul. She looked neither old nor young. Her skin was taut and bore a golden tan from many years spent outside. She had not an ounce of body fat on her and moved in graceful motion when she walked. Her dark hair was strewn with gray. She always wore it up, attached with an ivory comb that had been in her family for as long as she could remember. The intricate carving at the top was worn with age.

Diviña had buried two husbands, but much to her sorrow, had never been blessed with a child of her own. As leader of the Tinkers, she was matriarch to two nephews, the women they had married, and the five children that were her grandnieces and grandnephews. Traveling with the Tinkers was a boy of sixteen. Diviña had found the boy, unconscious, on the streets of Dublin when he was seven years old.

The year was 1839, and the family had set up camp in Dublin to participate in the summer solstice fair. Diviña was in a festive mood as she strolled through the fairgrounds. Slowly she meandered among stalls decorated brightly with flags and pennants flapping in the breeze. Buyers argued heatedly for the best prices with vendors selling copper kettles, brass trays, colored glass bottles of all shapes and sizes, pearls, ivory, and other semi-precious jewels. The air permeated with the pungent smells of aromatic spices from faraway lands, such as, ginger, paprika, and cinnamon. The Tinker woman delighted further at the aroma of meat roasting on spits, and pies stuffed with sausage, nutmeg, onions, and raisins. Young children roasted potatoes on sticks over an open fire. Diviña laughed as puppets charmed a small audience with their antics. She bought a bar of lavender soap, two needles, and some ribbons for her nieces' hair before returning to camp.

At the bottom of Cheap Street, she eyed a disturbance and considered taking another side street home. A band of older boys was beating the life out of a street urchin who lay huddled and bleeding on the cobblestone road. Something urged her to get involved. She quickly strode up to the boys and said, "Leave this child alone and be on your way!" Smirking, the biggest boy of the lot and quite clearly the leader, walked up to Diviña. He smelled of ale, and two of his top teeth were broken. Pushing and shoving each other, the boys left their prey and encircled Diviña.

"Look what we got here, lads. 'Tis the Tinker woman. Let's see what she brung us from the fair," the leader pronounced with a sneer. At that moment another boy came at Diviña from behind and snatched her scarf from around her neck.

"Move away from me, you hooligans," said Diviña, in a voice that sounded calmer than she felt. To her left, a lumbering movement caught her attention.

"I've warned you pack of rats to stay away from my pub. You're bad for business, and you upset my dear sainted mother," roared the voice from the largest man Diviña had ever seen. As he bellowed, he simultaneously began whacking the boys with the sturdy handle of a broom. The ruffians scattered in all directions, flapping their arms like a flock of birds that had been sprayed with buckshot.

"Are you alright, mistress?" asked the innkeeper.

"I am not harmed, but I fear this boy may be hurt. I have some skill with medicine, and I will tend to his wounds. Thank you for your help. You have been most kind." A light misty rain had begun to fall as Diviña walked over to where the small child lay moaning. He was barely conscious, and he bled from a gash at the back of his head.

The gigantic innkeeper bent down and gathered the lad in his arms. "It's starting to rain. You'd better come inside. It'll be easier for you to tend to his wounds."

"Sir, you are most kind, and that kindness will be repaid to you." Diviña picked up the desecrated scarf and her knapsack and followed the innkeeper into his establishment.

The pub was empty, except for an old man drinking his Guinness near the door. "I lose business when the fair is in town," explained the innkeeper. He set the boy on a heavy plank table and ambled to a back room to find some rags.

The inn was really no bigger than a large two-story cottage. It had rough wood floors covered with sawdust and a long oak bar that ran the length of one wall. Stairs led to a second floor where, Diviña guessed, the innkeeper lived with his mother and lodged the guests of the inn.

The patron of the inn appeared with a pail of water, a cake of soap and some towels. "This should clean the grime from his flesh so we can see what damage has been done. My name's Jack Harte, and I run this establishment with me mum. She's upstairs having a nap." Jack extended his large hand and Diviña shook it warmly.

"I am called Diviña. I'm camped with a troupe of Tinkers near the Ha Penny Bridge. We, too, are here for the fair."

The pair began the task by taking the boy's raggedy clothes off to survey the damage that had been inflicted to his body. The boy was so skinny, his skin rippled like a washboard against his ribs. Sores and bruises covered his legs and arms. He wore no shoes, and his feet were scarred and callused. Diviña studied the feet and commented to Jack that they looked enormously large compared to the rest of his body. There were scratches on his face, and the boy's right eye was red and puffy. Diviña knew the area would turn black and blue by morning. The blood, which had been streaming from the gash at the back of his head was already beginning to abate.

Diviña opened her knapsack and found the herbs she needed. "Lady's mantle will help stop the bleeding, and elder leaves will help stave off infection. He'll have a nasty bump for a while. If you would be kind enough to boil some water, Jack, I'll give him some birch bark tea when he comes around, and that will help the headache he's sure to have."

Jack began the task of boiling water, and together they scrubbed the filth and grime from the boy's body. They washed his hair and checked for lice. Amazingly, he had none. The boy had brown hair the color of dark tea. When Diviña checked his eyelids for mites, she saw that his eyes were the deepest shade of violet-blue that she had ever seen. He had long dark lashes, a short nose, and straight white teeth. By the time Diviña had completed the mission of uncovering the jewel of the boy buried in dirt, she knew that his path in life was destined to intertwine with hers. Jack found some clothes that had been left behind by one of his boarders, who had fled in the night for reasons unknown to Jack. The pants and shirt were too big, but the clothes were clean and far exceeded the rags the boy had been wearing.

"Would you join me in a cup of tea and some brown bread? My mother's a fair cook. I think you'll enjoy it," said Jack. He then proceeded to set a table with the bread, an assortment of cheeses, a pitcher of milk, and a steaming pot of tea.

Diviña found that she was hungry. The nutty cheese tasted rich and creamy, and the warm bread and tea gave her a feeling of contentment. "I hope you don't think I'm being too inquisitive, Jack, but have you not a wife?" she asked.

"When I was younger, I tried to court the village girls, but they just laughed at me and called me names like Goliath or ogre, sighed Jack. "After a while, I just gave up. I'm not complaining. I have a good life, and a mother who loves and needs me."

"Give me your hands, Jack," requested Diviña. "With your permission, I would like to tell your fortune to repay the kindness you have shown to me and the boy." Jack did as she asked. "I feel a wonderful warm strength, Jack, that comes from deep within you." Diviña was still for a moment. She said a silent prayer and closed her eyes to meditate. "I see that you will live a long and prosperous life, and that you will always be surrounded by those who care about you. In time, your mother will pass, in her sleep, to the heavens. You will be alone for one year. During that time, you will grieve for her daily, and it will be the saddest year of your life. You must go to the solstice fair the following summer and look for a woman wearing a purple shawl. I see red hair, and eyes the color of topaz. She sells woolen cloth from Donegal. Go to her Jack. She is your destiny. And when she smiles at you, she sees the strength and beauty that live inside your soul." Diviña opened her eyes and smiled at Jack.

"I don't know if what you say is true, mistress, but I just had a light-headed feeling like the rush of too much ale gone to my head," whispered Jack as he shuddered.

At that moment the boy started to stir. "Where am I? I feel so warm and clean, this must be heaven." The boy groaned. When he tried to sit up he winced with pain. "Ouch! My head feels like a herd of cattle trampled over it."

Jack and Diviña gave the boy the birch bark tea, and he slept for another hour. When he awoke again, they fed him some bread, cheese and a cup of tea while he told them what he knew of his life.

"I never knew my parents. For as long as I can remember, I lived with an old crone named Mary Corcoran. She was called Shady Mary because she was blind in one eye and had a hard time seeing. She said she found me in a pile of rubbish outside the town of Kildare, and reckoned that I was about a year old. Shady Mary had me baptized by a priest she met on the road a few days later. If I died, she did not want it on her conscience that I might still be a heathen baby and float forever in limbo. She told the priest to christen me John, for my first name, because she didn't want me to have a fancier name than her, and Martin Corcoran for the rest, in memory of her father. We lived by our wits on the road. Shady Mary taught me how to pick pockets from the people who went to the village fairs. She was straight with me. She fed me when I was useful, and beat me when I didn't pull in my share of the booty. Shady Mary was robbed and killed when I was six. I found her by the side of the road, and buried her in that very spot for there was naught else I could do. I have lived, for a year now, practicing the skills she taught me," the boy proclaimed without emotion.

"Why were those boys beating you?" asked Diviña.

"They saw me steal a few coins off the table from one of the stalls as the owner was bargaining with a customer. They followed me to this place and jumped me. They robbed me, and told me that they were going to beat the life out of me for trespassing on their territory," said John in a matter-of-fact tone.

Diviña was enchanted by the boy's straightforward account of his miserable life. He was neither bitter nor cynical about the fate that had been handed to him. It was easy to see that John was cheerful by nature. That he was intelligent, was obvious. Against all odds, he had not only survived but had prospered, until today. His story only strengthened her feeling that their lives were meant to interlock. When she asked him if he would like to come and live with her, he did not hesitate in saying yes.

Together they formed a bond as strong as any mother and son. They had not been together a month when John began calling her mother. It seemed as natural to Diviña as it did to him.

When John turned nine, he had a different request. "Mam?" asked John, "I've been thinking about something, and I want to know what you think."

Diviña could tell that the boy was troubled about something. "Come here John, and sit by me," she requested as she cooked a pan of wild mushrooms she had gathered in the woods. "What's wrong? Has someone been unkind to you?"

"Oh no, 'tis just that I was wondering about my name and all," he said.

"Your name? John is a lovely name, and St. John was our Lord's favorite apostle."

"No Mam, not my first name, I like the name John, and I like Martin too. 'Tis my last name, Corcoran. 'Tis, well...'tis different from everybody else in our troupe," he said slowly. "I thought maybe I might like to change my last name."

"Oh," said Diviña thoughtfully, "I have given this very subject some thought over the two years we've been together, John. Son, I know that your time with Shady Mary was hard, and that you've been happier since you came to live with us. But, Mary did save you from certain death by plucking you off of that heap of rubbish. For all the bad things that she taught you, she did think enough about you to have a priest baptize you, and she gave you her surname. She must have loved you more than you know."

John laughed. "Mam, she was Shady Mary. She couldn't see any longer to practice her trade. I became her eyes."

"That may well be true, but still, I'm grateful to her for keeping you alive. Shady Mary played a large part in bringing you to me. If you take the name I carry now, it will be the name of a man you never met. And if you take my maiden name, our names will still be different. John Martin Corcoran is a fine Irish name. I have a feeling that you will have many descendants who will proudly carry that name. I think that Shady Mary would want it to be so."

And so their life continued. Diviña taught John how to read. He read anything he could get his hands on. His favorites were the stories of the Knights of the Round Table and King Arthur. Diviña explained that King Arthur was an ancient Celt from the Welsh tribes. Diviña taught John how to juggle five balls. He possessed a natural talent for music. He had a strong clear voice, and could play haunting Irish tunes on the whistle. He learned to play the fiddle from his uncles, and soon he could play better than anyone in the troupe. His gift in spinning a good yarn around the campfire captivated all who knew him. He was popular in the towns and villages they toured, particularly with the lasses. John had a keen wit. He loved to tease Diviña and the rest of his family. He ate like a horse, and in time, his body toned to an athlete's build. Years of setting up tents and breaking them down, and chopping and hauling wood for campfires made him strong. His shoulders and arms were as powerful as granite boulders. By the age of sixteen John had reached a height of six feet and two inches and weighed sixteen stone. Finally, the once scrawny boy, who had been rescued outside Jack Harte's Pub, had grown into proportion with his outlandishly large feet. John loved Diviña as much as any son could ever love his mother. He was fiercely protective of her. Finding each other completed them both, and their life together was full.

Chapter 9 ~ June 1848 - Dellamort Wood

"Mam, I thought I might go into the woods and poach us a couple of pheasant for our evening meal. There's nothing on this earth as fine as a juicy roasted pheasant, and that bit of forest there is ripe for the taking. I heard them squawking as we were setting up camp," added John as he packed his satchel with a slingshot, some round stones, and various other items that he might need.

"Take your knitted woolen. The June air can still get nippy at dusk," instructed Diviña.

"Mam, I'm sixteen and a grown man," laughed John.

"You may be sixteen, John Martin Corcoran, but I still know what's best for my son." Diviña teased. "What time do you think you might be back?"

"With luck, I hope to return in about an hour with a couple of fat birds for the spit."

"Be on the lookout for keepers, John. The owner of that estate will not be wanting any of his pheasant taken by the likes of us, and I know the place will be guarded," she cautioned.

"Have I ever had my backside peppered with buckshot, Mam?" John asked. "You know I'm as swift and silent as a leopard on a hunt." John lifted Diviña off the ground and growled into her neck. "Get the fire ready, we'll be feasting tonight," John called as he headed off in the direction of Dellamort Wood.

John looked at the sky. He reckoned that he had about an hour before the sun would set. He understood that it was important to poach the pheasant before it became dark. When the sun went down, he knew the pheasant would fly up into the trees to roost for the night, and it would be too late.

What I need is a lovely open meadow or a clearing where 'tis not too wooded, he thought. John knew that the pheasant on this land would be easy pickings. They, most likely, were raised for hunting parties given by the owner of the estate. Pheasant hunts were quite popular among the aristocrats. John also knew that keepers usually fed them on a diet of meal, and that most were probably half-tame already. He always carried a supply of cornmeal in his satchel to lure the birds closer for an easier target with his slingshot.

John threaded his way carefully through a wooded shrub area. Up ahead he could see a wide path that was well worn with wagon tracks and horse hooves. He did not want to use the path in case the keepers were guarding the property. The last thing the eager young hunter wanted was buckshot in his rump. It had been drizzling most of the day, and he hoped that the keepers had gone home to a warm fire. He moved gracefully through the leaves, barely making a sound. Long shadows lent a mysterious mood to his surroundings as the day slowly ebbed to the dusk of twilight. John scanned the area with his eyes and could see a large meadow and a lake in the far distance. Suddenly, he tensed and came to a stop. The faint whimpering sound of an animal caught his ear. His first thought was that a small animal had, perhaps, been caught in a trap. He listened more closely. Clearly, it was the soft whimpering moans of a dog. He wondered if some poor unlucky dog had been lured by bait, and was caught in a metal trap meant for some other animal. He had seen it happen before.

"Here fella, nice puppy, come here boy," John coaxed in soothing tones. He did not want to frighten a dog, which most likely was already scared half to death. Moving closer to the sound of the frightened dog, John brushed aside some low branches to see a small black and white dog, with a rope leash around its neck, covering the upper body of a young girl who appeared to be dead or unconscious. The dog was licking her face. It was clear that the girl was in critical condition, and the agitated dog sensed this.

"Come here, fella, I won't hurt you," John said in a soft reassuring whisper. The dog seemed grateful someone had come along. He trotted over to where the man had squatted down and allowed John to pet him. Then an amazing thing happened. The dog put his mouth over John's hand in an effort to lead him to where the young girl lay crumpled. John let the dog take him to the girl, and immediately he knew that this girl was in grave trouble. He bent over her lifeless body and put his hand on her neck to see if she was alive. He could barely feel the faint beating of a pulse. She was deathly cold. John examined her head. The girl had lost a tremendous amount of blood from a large gash at the back of her head. The tide of blood was no longer flowing, but he knew that if she did not get immediate attention she probably would not live. John had the sense that she would have been dead already had it not been for her dog. The dog had obviously tried to cover the girl with his fur to help keep her warm.

"You're pretty smart, little lad," praised John. The dog stood up on his haunches and barked. "I know. We've got to get her out of these damp clothes." John knew he had to make some preparations before moving the girl. He ripped off the large cotton scarf tied around his neck. He carefully wrapped it around her head to keep the blood from flowing when he began to move her about. Quickly, he removed the hand-knitted woolen Diviña had made for him last winter and wrapped it around her body. He secured the garment by knotting the sleeves together. "Let's get her some help, little fella," said John as he bent down and lifted the girl into his arms. He gathered the leash off the ground and motioned the little dog to come with him. The dog appeared happy to leave the area.

As he headed back in the direction of the camp, John made the decision to take his chances with the main path to make better time. The girl felt as light as a wisp in his arms. Her icy-cold flesh pressed against his chest and he shuddered. *Diviña, I've got to get her to Mam. She'll know what to do.* Bailey followed the steps of the anxious young man carrying his mistress in the opposite direction of the Dellamort Manor.

Chapter 10 ~ June 1848 - Tinker Encampment

Diviña sat by a large fire roasting onions when she heard John frantically call her name. She jumped up and ran in the direction of his voice.

"Mam, Mam," "here's a girl I found near dead in the woods. She's terribly hurt," John gasped in a voice that was winded and shaken.

Diviña took one look at the unconscious lass and sprang to action. "Quickly, John, bring her into the caravan and lay her on the lower bunk."

John raced up the steps of the caravan, and gently placed the girl on the bed. Diviña felt her pulse. "Her flesh is as cold as frost, John. We must get her under these quilts to bring her temperature up. Help me get her shoes off." John did as he was asked. Bailey had followed the pair through the open door of the caravan and stood whining by the door. "John, what's that dog going on about?"

"I found the girl bleeding to death in the woods, Mam, and I think she'd be dead already had it not been for this little dog. 'Twas the cries of the pup that led me to the lass. 'Tis a miracle I found her. She was in a very woodsy area, and had been bleeding from that large gash at the back of her head. Mam, there was something very odd about the whole situation, for I could find naught around her to have caused the wound. It almost seemed like she'd been placed there to die. I didn't have time to look about, for I knew it was vital to bring her to you, but I've a nagging suspicion there's foul play concerning this child."

Diviña attended to the girl as John talked. She removed the scarf. Large areas of blood had dried and matted the hair to her scalp. "Find my scissors in my medical sack. I will need to cut away a portion of her hair so I can tend to her wound. I'm going to have to stitch the wound closed with my needle and twine. Son, there's water boiling in the kettle. Bring it to me, and get the cake of soap near the bucket. I'll want to clean the gash before I sew the cut closed."

"Yes, Mam," answered John. He rushed down the caravan steps to do what Diviña had requested.

When John returned with the kettle and soap, he observed that Diviña had already cut away part of the girl's hair. The gash was about two inches in length and very deep. "Do you want me to still her head while you sew her up, Mam?" asked John. He had assisted Diviña on a number of occasions by holding a patient who needed to have a rotten tooth pulled or a cut sewn closed. He was not squeamish about blood.

"That would be a big help, son, but frankly I do not think she'll feel a thing. The lass will be lucky if she makes it through the night. We'll do what we can for her, John, then all we can do is pray. She's in the hands of God."

Diviña cleaned the wound with the hot soapy water, and deftly stitched the gaping wound closed. She made a poultice of lavender and lady's mantle to stem the flow of further bleeding and help prevent the wound from becoming infected. She and John took turns sitting up with the girl throughout the night. John insisted on taking the first watch. "John, I've made a strong tea of lavender leaves and birch bark. Make sure you give it to her if she happens to wake up. It will help her pain and reduce the swelling."

Tara did not stir during the night, or into the next day. John and Diviña continued to change her bandages and apply the poultice. "Shouldn't she be wakin' up soon, Mam?" asked John.

Her pulse is stronger than it once was, and I believe her color is improving. The body is a remarkable instrument, son. What the lass needs is rest, and that's what nature is telling her to do. She's still a little feverish, but I am certain that, too, will improve. This girl has been through an ordeal, John, and I'm not just talking about the incident in the woods. I feel certain that she's come to us for a reason. It is our duty to protect her from all harm. Surely, she's been sent to us by the saints in heaven." John nodded as he stared at the young girl sleeping in his mother's bed.

Several miles away, Squire Chase Dellamort sat in his morning room conferencing with Nevil Hawkins. "What do you mean, the search party cannot find the girl!" he croaked through clenched teeth. He lowered his voice and added, "I gave you specific instructions where I left her. Are you certain you steered them in the right direction?" The squires right eye flared an odd shade of yellow

"Sir, I was with them and saw first hand as they searched the area completely. Nevil was quite agitated as he spoke. We found remnants of blood in the woody area, but all traces of the girl had vanished. Her satchel was gone, as well as her little dog."

"Well, she can't have gone far in the condition she was in. Continue to look for her. I want that girl found! I'll not have a child making a fool of me. She *will* be captured and brought back to my estate. The fact that she tried to run away will make her look extremely unfavorable in the eyes of the constable," lectured the squire. "Have you questioned the staff?"

"Yes, sir. I gathered them together early this morning, and told them of the theft of the silver. I informed them that Mary was witness to the incident. They were quite upset when I told them that the girl had made a run for it. Naturally, I didn't mention the accident. I asked if any of them knew where she might have gone. The Curran girl mentioned that Tara was on very friendly terms with a village priest called Father Scanlon. She may well have tried to get to him. With your permission, sir, I believe we might want to make a visit to the priest."

"Indeed, Nevil. That's a good idea. After all, the child had no money and no food to speak of. She could not have gone far. Someone must be helping her. This afternoon we will make a visit to the priest.

If he's trying to harbor the girl, we'll soon get it out of him," the squire announced. "Let's bring the constable along in case the priest tries to get clever with us."

Tara awoke just as the sun was beginning to set. The back of her head pounded like a mallet beating against a drum. The pain blurred her vision, and it took some time to focus her eyes to her surroundings. Tara saw a young man on a chair resting his head on a small wooden table. He looked large. Almost out of place in his surroundings. Tara thought, *Where am I? This hut is very small.* She slowly took in all that was around her. The little room was long and narrow. A small iron stove rested against one of the walls. *The owner must use it for cooking and heating.* A cleverly built metal chimney extended up and through a curved roof to filter smoke from the stove to the outside. Next to the stove, she saw a tiny sink and shelves attached to the walls. Everything in the hut was neat and orderly. The glow of a flame from a brass oil lamp hung from a hook attached to an L-shape bracket. It was bolted to the wall near the sink. The lamp illuminated the room with soft golden light. *'Tis so strange. I feel safe here. Safer than I've felt in a long time.* Tara noticed Bailey asleep at the foot of her bed. *My clothes?* Tara realized that she was wearing a white cotton nightgown that did not belong to her.

All at once Tara's eyes were drawn to the glow of a beautiful blue bottle resting on a corner shelf at the far end of the hut near a small door. The bottle was the most magnificent thing Tara had ever seen in her entire life. It appeared to be about ten inches tall. The shape of the bottle was somewhat ordinary. Tara had seen Nevil serve drinks to the squire and his guests at the gala from similar bottles. The bottle was round and fat on the bottom with a small narrow neck and a round stopper shaded in the same brilliant blue tones. *The color of this bottle is so vibrant and lovely. I am drawn to it like a moth to the flame. It's as though the bottle releases its glow from an inner source. But...that cannot be. I must be with the fever to think 'tis so.* Tara could not take her eyes from the bottle, so she studied it some more. *The bottle looks to have been painted. Many shades of sapphire blue with silver are layered in swirls of a shiny jewel-like pigment. I've never, in my life, seen anything so shiny and brilliant. It's colors remind me of pictures I have seen of the ocean.* As Tara stared at the bottle, its color seemed to change ever so slightly as though it was a living thing. *I know it cannot be so, but I seem to gather strength from the light of this bottle. I feel there is a healing going on inside me as I drink from its beauty.*

"Well you've finally come back to us from the dead," said a voice from afar.

Tara had been so entranced by the beauty of the bottle she startled at the voice, which reminded her that she was not alone in the hut. She shuddered. The action woke Bailey at the end of the bed. In an instance, he was up near her face licking her neck and chin. Tara tried to speak to the dog, but found all she could manage was a hoarse whisper.

The voice moved his chair closer to the bunk where Tara lay petting her dog. She realized it was the same boy who had been sleeping with his head on the table. "You gave Mam and me quite a scare," he began speaking rapidly. "I found you near dead in the forest. Your dog was barking and that led me to you." Bailey moved to the edge of the bed and began to lick the boy's hands. "This little pup saved your life. He covered you with his body to keep you warm. I carried you out of the woods and brought you here last night. That was nearly twenty-four hours ago. We were beginning to think you might never wake up." Tara tried to follow the lad but the words came so fast and her head still pounded. It was hard to think clearly. "I'm going to run and fetch Mam," he said with a lively voice. "She'll be happy to know that you're out of the woods...not out of the woods where I found you, but...well...you know. I'll be right back." Tara watched in confusion as the young man ducked his head low to dash out the small door.

A moment later, a woman entered the room and smiled. She had the most loving look in her eyes. Tara was instantly drawn to her. The woman walked over to the bed and felt Tara's forehead with her hand. "My name is Diviña, and this is my son John. We've been very worried about you, and are glad that you are finally...out of the woods." Diviña smiled and winked at John. Tara had the feeling that the mother and son were sharing something between them, but she was confused as to what it might be. Tara tried to speak, but the words would not come out clearly. Her parched throat felt like the newly plowed dust in Da's fields, and her tongue seemed swollen like a loaf of her mother's yeast-dough ready for baking. "I'm very thirsty," was all she could manage.

"I will make you some herbed tea. It will soothe the dryness in your mouth and help with the pain. Can you sit up?"

Tara nodded but found that she could not will her muscles to obey her mind.

"John, would you be kind enough to help the lass sit up? Give her a sip of water and amuse her with one of your stories while I make the healing tea."

John reached for Tara and lifted her frail form to an upright position and adjusted the pillows to support her head. He marveled that her body felt so warm in his arms, in contrast to the cold lifeless form he had carried from the woods. Carefully, John placed the cup of water to her lips as he described the events that led him to finding her in the woods and his decision to bring her to their camp.

The cold sweet water trickled down Tara's throat building her strength much like the plants she had fed with compost and watered so lovingly in the squire's garden.

Diviña insisted that Tara drink all the herbal tea before she would allow her to talk. She applied a new compress of calendula and lavender to ease the painful swelling at the back of her head. A knock on the door caused Tara to jump, but it was only Diviña's nephews bringing a large pot of stew and a crusty loaf of bread that had been made by their wives. The savory broth warmed Tara, and she felt her strength return with each sip of the hot nourishing liquid.

John wondered, *What has happened to this lass to make her so fearful?*

It took several hours for Tara to relay the events of the past year, but by late evening John and Diviña had a sense of the loneliness and hardship the girl had endured working on the estate. When her story ended, Tara implored, "You've been more than kind to me, but I must leave here tonight. Squire Dellamort is a very powerful man. The squire and his butler are surely looking for me. I'm certain that they'll not rest 'til they bring me back to the estate. They, most likely, have enlisted the help of the constable. It's only a matter of time before they track me to this place. I do not want to get you in trouble. If you could bring me my clothes, I'll leave tonight and you'll not be in danger."

John and Diviña looked at each other. At length, it was Diviña who spoke. "It is clear that you must get away from this area, and I promise you that John and I will do all we can to assist you on your journey. But you have had a nasty cut and are still very weak. Please trust us, that we know what's best for you."

John added, "Sleep here tonight. 'Tis late, and I doubt anyone will come looking for you at this hour. Tomorrow we'll make plans to get you out of the area. Rest easy tonight, lass." Tara thanked Diviña and John. She knew it would be foolish to try and leave before she was able. At length, John excused himself for the night.

"I can't take your bed, where will you sleep?" questioned Tara.

"I prefer to sleep under the stars, especially on a fine night like this, but we also carry extra tents so don't worry about me, lass. You and Mam can have the caravan tonight." He grinned as he turned to leave through the small door.

When John closed the door, Diviña set about cleaning up the dishes from their dinner. Tara again found her focus drawn to the shimmering bottle on the shelf. "Excuse me, Mistress, I can't help but admire the lovely bottle that rests on the shelf in the corner. I'm drawn to its beauty, and the peaceful feeling I get when I look at it. I've never seen anything so beautiful. Even Granny Cassie's Belleek would pale in its shadow…and the color…well 'tis almost as though 'tis alive with a spirit unto itself."

Diviña listened to Tara's description of the bottle and smiled knowingly. She stepped across the caravan to the shelf and gathered the bottle in her hands. Still smiling, Diviña walked over to Tara's bed and reverently placed the azure-colored bottle into the girl's hands. A feeling of warmth spread from Tara's fingers to every part of her body, and without realizing it, large tears fell from a face that was radiant with joy. In time, she composed herself and said, "You must forgive me, Mistress. I do know not what manner of behavior this is. I must be overwrought with all that has happened to me these past days."

"You have nothing to be embarrassed about, lass. It sometimes happens, that *this particular* bottle can stimulate various emotions in certain people." Diviña pulled the chair John had been sitting in closer to Tara and spoke. "Tara, I would like to tell you what I know about this bottle and how it came into my hands."

Diviña settled into the chair and began to tell her tale. "Four years ago our little band was camped near the small village of Lahinch near Liscannor Bay. We had gone to County Clare for a large musical festival in the area. Naturally, we set up our tents to practice our craft and make the small income with which to satisfy our earthly needs. One day, a man came into my tent to have his fortune told. He was a tall handsome man with black hair and skin the color of roasted chestnuts. His name was Yasser Abdul-Razek, and he was in his mid-thirties. He was very likable and had a quick smile, which made his large brown eyes sparkle. Yasser was an Arabian exporter from an ancient city called Mombassa near the coast of East Africa. The handsome Arab had sailed to many exotic places, from that port off the Indian Ocean, to buy and sell goods for profit. He enjoyed his work very much, but I sensed something was troubling him.

"Yasser told me that he was looking to find his younger brother whom he had lost nearly a year ago when a violent storm separated their ships at sea. He wished to know if I might be able to help him. I asked if he had any article of clothing or any other item from his brother's possessions."

Tara looked perplexed so Diviña added, "Often a personal item, which is important to the friend or relative can help assist me with my visions." She continued, "Yasser had in his sea bag a woven scarf, which was a favorite of his brother's, and I used this item to guide me in my revelations. I beheld that his brother had indeed survived the storm at sea, but his broken ship had washed up on a small island off the coast of Morocco. I told the young man that I felt confident that his brother was alive, and I gave him two numbers, which meant nothing to me, but I had a strong feeling that they might mean something to him. Yasser was certain that the two numbers were navigational directions, and he felt confident that I had put him on the correct path.

"The next afternoon Yasser appeared at my tent and said he would be leaving the next day, with the morning tide, to go in search of his brother. He said he had heard of a lovely stretch of bluffs called the Cliffs of Moher, which he wanted to see before he left. He asked me if I might take a ride to the cliffs to share a lunch he had prepared and to enjoy the day with him. I was happy to spend time in his company. He had been to numerous places on his journeys and had met many interesting people. It was enlightening to hear about his life. The cliffs were spectacular, and we settled on a blanket to enjoy the meal he had prepared for us. It was then that he pulled from his sea bag the most beautiful bottle I had ever seen.

"The surface of the bottle was ablaze with brilliant patches of red, amber, and orange. Small streaks of blue raced across its surface like a river searching to find its course. The unusual bottle seemed to possess the same internal radiance of the sun, which was shimmering its light upon the sea. Yasser placed the bottle in my hands, and I was blinded by the purity of its beauty. It gave me an enhanced sense of peace and tranquility. Suddenly, I thought my eyes were playing tricks on me or that perhaps it was the influence of sun sparkling on the water, but the bottle began to change ever so slightly in color. Mixed within the warm shades of amber and red, streaks of blue began swirling with other shades of sapphire and aqua much like the currents in the sea. I looked at him with amazement and he smiled. Yasser told me that the bottle had come into his keeping in exactly the same manner that it was coming to me. I was very confused, so he enlightened me. I remember every word that he spoke to me, as though our conversation happened only yesterday," relayed Diviña with a faraway look in her eyes.

"Yasser had explained patiently to me, that the origin of his bottle was unknown, but he knew that it was ancient. He said the bottle appeared to be made of glass, but its surface had been colored over with layers of a hard glossy covering. I mean, layers and layers of a shiny bright jewel-like substance. Once on a visit to Bombay, he encountered an East Indian spice trader, and it was he who gave him the bottle. It was a rich shade of cinnamon intermixed with patches of gold the first time he laid eyes on it. The spice trader told him that he had received the bottle from a young nun working at an orphanage in Calcutta. The purpose of the bottle appears to be such, that it helps people who are on a journey to find their way. During our meeting yesterday, he shared that he began to suspect that the bottle was changing when he reached into his sea bag to give me his brother's scarf. He told me that his intuition was confirmed later in the evening as he witnessed the transformation of color changing before his very eyes. He said the blue streaks had never been there before. He then knew, the time had come to pass the bottle into my keeping, and thanks to me, his journey to find his brother must nearly be over." Diviña's body gave a little shudder, and the gesture seemed to bring her memories of that day to the present.

"Tara, everything that Yasser told me that day on the cliffs came true. The bottle finds its owner and when this happens the exterior surface begins to change. Outer layers of new pigments replace the existing colors. And although this may be hard to understand, I believe that the bottle takes on the spirit or personality of the person it comes to be with, and together they begin a personal voyage or a journey. The Sapphire Bottle has been most useful to me in the time it has been in my possession, but now it has chosen to come to you, Tara, and it will help you on your journey. If you look closely, you may notice that shades of emerald green are beginning to appear in places. I know that this is hard to comprehend, but do you believe what I am saying?"

"'Tis strange," said Tara, "but all that you're telling me makes perfect sense, even though logically...scientifically...I know it should not."

"You must understand, Tara, this is not a genie bottle that will grant you wishes like in the *Tales of the Arabian Nights*, but it does have certain mystical powers, and it will assist you in your future endeavors. You must trust that the bottle will help you find what you're looking for. The bottle will also help you assist others who are in need to find their way. Then, one day, someone will come into your life and the color of the bottle will change once again. When this happens, you will know that it's time to pass the bottle into the keeping of another good person who has greater need of it than you."

Tara looked at the bottle, which was resting in her lap. In the last thirty minutes it was clearly evident, that the bottle was changing in color. Patches of emerald, moss, jade, and gold were gradually covering the beautiful shades of sapphire blue. She studied the bottle further, and asked, "Diviña, what's this writing on the bottom edge of the bottle? It looks to be an inscription in Latin."

"Yes, you're right, the words are in Latin. It is a poem, child, inscribed in beautiful calligraphy in the form of a couplet." Diviña recited the English translation for Tara.

Into thy hand I come.
Unto thy spirit as one.

Chapter 11 ~ June 1848 - Tinker Encampment

That night Tara slept more peacefully than she had in a very long time. She dreamed that Grandma Cassie had written a note to her on delicate parchment paper rolled into a scroll that had been placed inside the stunning bottle. She carefully unrolled the scroll to reveal her words written in beautiful calligraphy. The content of the message was simple. It read:

Tara, I love you.
I will see you, someday.
Granny Cassie.

A strong sense of peace settled in Tara's heart and she awoke smiling. In her little shed, she usually tossed fitfully as she slept and awoke feeling tired. Last night, the warmth of the bed wrapped her like a gentle summer breeze. *'Tis odd but I feel safe among these strangers.* The pounding at the back of her head was gone. She looked around the caravan and discovered that she was alone. Even Bailey had deserted her. The bottle had been placed back in its corner, and when Tara looked at it again, it was clear that the variegated blues on the surface were becoming overlaid with many shades of green. Tara sat up and saw that a clean set of clothes and undergarments had been laid out for her at the bottom of the bed. Slowly, she stood and dressed herself in a brightly colored purple and green tweed skirt, a white linen blouse, a black woolen vest with lacing across the front, and a crocheted lavender shawl. Cotton stockings and a pair of black leather boots completed the outfit. She dressed, then carefully made the bed and poked her head out the caravan door.

The entire troupe of Tinkers was sharing a morning meal around their campfire. John held Bailey on his lap as he drank from a steaming mug of tea. He looked at her and said protectively, "Are you sure you should be out of bed?" Diviña smiled. She walked to where the young girl stood, and escorted her over to the group. The woodsy smoke from the fire was warm and inviting. Introductions were made all around, and Diviña guided Tara off to a place where she might take care of her natural needs and freshen herself with some water.

"Tara, I'm happy that your condition is so much improved, but it's not safe for you to be outside. Let me accompany you back to the caravan, and John will bring you some bread and tea."

"I cannot thank you for your kindness, but if you'll give me back my clothes, Bailey and I will not trouble you further. There is grave danger in what you are doing," she added fearfully.

"These clothes are my gift to you, and I must say they suit you quite well. The ones you were wearing were fairly ruined, and we burned all traces of them in the fire. I'm afraid you'll have to make do with these."

Tara professed, "I have never worn anything as beautiful as these fine garments in my life. How can I ever repay your kindness?"

"There is no need. I have always believed that the good things we do for others will come back to us in time. And those who commit cruel and cunning deeds will one day be held accountable for their actions. It is the natural order of things."

Diviña led Tara up the steps and into the caravan. "With all my heart, I hope that what you say is true," said Tara earnestly. "Perhaps, one day, the cruelty of those two men will become exposed for others to see. I can forgive them for what they did to me and my family, but I am tortured with the thought that Shauna and Danny must continue to suffer at their hands."

"The squire and his butler are truly cruel and arrogant men, and those must be the sins that sadden our Lord the most," she stated sadly. "Someday, they will be held accountable for the brutal acts which they have inflicted upon you and others. It is written in the stars," she proclaimed smiling.

John entered the caravan and handed Tara a thick slice of warm bread slathered with honey and a steaming mug of tea. Bailey settled at Tara's feet and curled himself into a fluffy ball. Tara devoured every morsel of the food.

John scratched his head and uttered, "I must say, you look exceedingly better than when I carried you out of the woods."

At that moment, the sound of horses' hooves broke the discussion inside the caravan. Voices could be heard in loud conversation with Diviña's nephews as John and Diviña sprang swiftly into action. John handed Bailey into Tara's arms, and lifted the mattress and its wooden platform up on hinges to reveal a hidden compartment under the bed. He silently motioned to Tara with his hands what he wanted her to do and helped her and Bailey clamber inside. Diviña snatched the curious bottle from its shelf and thrust it into Tara hands along with her satchel. It took but a minute for Tara and Bailey to be safely hidden inside the box. The false bottom was closed just as the sound of loud knocking thundered against the caravan door.

Calmly, Diviña opened the door. A small wiry man wearing fawn colored riding breeches, black boots, and carrying a riding crop abruptly entered the caravan uninvited. He scanned the room. At the far end of the caravan, he saw a tall young man sitting on the lower edge of a bunk bed drinking tea. "My name is Squire Chase Dellamort. I'm looking for a fugitive," he began curtly. "One of my servant girls stole some valuable silver from me and absconded into the night with it two days ago. We think she may be hurt and, therefore, still in the area. The constable is outside and has authorized me to search this camp. Have you any knowledge of this thief?"

"We only arrived here recently ourselves," said Diviña calmly, "and most of our time has been spent setting up camp. What does the girl look like, and what makes you think she's hurt?"

The squire darted a look toward Diviña thinking he may have offered too much information. He ignored the latter part of her question. "She is thin...with dark hair and the eyes...I don't know the color!" he shouted irritably. "She worked as one of many servants on my estate. I can't say that I paid much attention to her." The squire's eyes darted in all directions of the caravan as he spoke. It was clear that he was not impressed with the cramped quarters of its interior.

John smiled at the squire as he spoke, "'Twill keep our eyes and ears open, and if we should hear anythin', we'll gladly pass this information on to your lordship. Now, might you be offerin' a small reward for this knowledge that you seem to prize so dearly?" he intoned in mock deference to the squire.

Chase Dellamort eyed the muscular young man suspiciously. He had the feeling that the lad was being overly polite, and he did not like the pasty smile on the boy's face, but he favored the idea of a reward if it might entice someone to turn her over to him. "I will pay a handsome reward of twenty quid to anyone who leads me to the lass. By the way, you're trespassing on my private land, and I wish you to vacate the area immediately."

"Actually, this is public land," proclaimed John. "We checked with the constable when we arrived in the village. Your land is bordered across the road. But, in truth, we have tired of this place and are thinking of moving on in a few days anyway. A fair begins to the north in Monaghan next week, doesn't it, Mam?"

"I believe it does, son."

Dellamort knew that the young man was correct about the public land. He was beginning to feel claustrophobic and had grown impatient with the Tinkers. He turned angrily on the heel of his boot and banged his head slightly as he charged out the low caravan door.

John rose to follow the squire out the door. A man, whom he recognized as the constable, was talking to a small-boned man with a beak nose that matched Tara's description of the odious butler. The riders, having finished the inspections of the three caravans, mounted their horses and rode away.

When John entered the caravan, Diviña was assisting the fugitives out of the hidden compartment. Tara was shaking uncontrollably, and her face was as white as parchment paper. "The sound of that man's voice sends shivers up my spine," she whispered. John handed her the mug of tea, but it shook so violently in her hand that he took it and gently placed it on the table. At length, she composed herself. "'Tis the strangest thing. Bailey has never liked being closed up in small places, but the second you put the bottle into my hand and shut the door, he fell asleep and never moved a muscle. Then, the moment you opened the latch and took the bottle he woke up." Tara looked down at the dog that was now sitting quietly in her lap.

Diviña smiled, "The bottle can sometimes have a calming effect in certain situations, when the need arises."

Tara looked at the bottle shimmering so brightly on the table and shook her head in wonder. The bottle somehow calmed her and she felt her heart rate begin to slow back to normal.

"John, it's obvious that Tara is in grave danger. You must take your horse, Maggie, and ride to Dublin with Tara tonight. Go to Jack Harte's inn. He will help you both get on board a ship to North America. Jack knows many people. I am certain he will be able to help you," she assured.

John looked at his mother and understood what she meant without any further words passing between them. "Are you certain that *this* is the best plan? Once I get the lass on a ship, surely that's the extent of where our help is needed."

Tara could clearly see that John was not happy about the arrangements his mother was making, and protested. "I am fully capable of finding my own way home to my family. Give me the street address of your friend Jack, and I will work to earn my passage on board a ship."

Diviña turned to John and spoke in soft tones, "John, I believe that it is our duty and our destiny to assist this lass in returning to her family. She *could* possibly do this alone, but I believe it would be better if you, son, were to help her on this journey. When she has been safely reunited with her family, you may return to me, if that is your wish.

"Of course it's my wish!" said John angrily. He did not talk for several moments. He sat staring out a small window in the caravan looking very unhappy. Finally he turned to his mother and spoke. "I will do this favor at your request, out of respect for you, Mam," John expressed in a tone that barely masked his unhappiness.

"Thank you, John. Now, I must ask one more favor of you. Before this unwelcome intrusion by the squire, Tara and I were talking. She feels that her friends must be worried sick about her. She asked me if you could get to a stable boy, named Danny, and let him know she is okay. You can tell him that she'll be leaving on board a ship out of Dublin and not to worry about her."

Tara added, "I know this is a lot to ask, but Danny always picks up the horses from the north paddock at three o'clock in the afternoon. I think I can tell you a way to get to him without drawing attention to yourself."

John looked at Tara and chuckled, "Now this is a task that is well within my range of expertise, lass." John turned to his mother and laughed. "If there was one thing I learned from Shady Mary, it was how to slip in and out of places without drawing attention to myself."

"Who's Shady Mary?" asked Tara.

John and Diviña smiled. "I'll tell you about her on the ride to Dublin, lass," said John.

It was nearly midnight when John and Tara were packed and ready to go. Diviña had cleverly made a knapsack for Bailey to ride in so Tara's arms would be free to steady herself on the horse. John's mare, Maggie, was a sturdy black and white paint he had bought with money saved from three seasons of work. She was a gentle horse and well taken care of. It had been decided that John would leave the horse in Dublin with Jack until he returned, or until the troupe might make its way to the city. The Tinker women had packed food for the eighty-mile journey. It was only a small amount because the pair were riding double and needed to travel light.

"You should be able to make it as far as Louth by morning," advised Diviña. "John, remember that lovely glen and stream we camped at two summers ago?" John nodded. "Rest there for the day out of sight. Proceed to Drogheda in the evening, and from there, the road to Dublin is an easy day's ride. You should be at Jack's in two to three days depending on the weather."

Tara turned and faced the band of Tinkers who had risked so much for her. "No words can express my thanks for all the kindness you've shown me. You've risked your lives for a stranger. I'll never forget you, and you will always be in my prayers." She hugged everyone, and turned to face Diviña. "How can I thank you, Diviña? You have lent me your only son to help me on this journey. I'm truly humbled by your generous nature," said Tara choked with emotion.

Diviña placed the bottle in Tara's hands. It was encased in a soft leather pouch with a long sturdy strap of the same leather. "Place this strap across your neck and under your shoulder, and the bottle should be well protected as you ride," instructed Diviña. "Do not be afraid, child. The bottle will guide you on your journey home." The two women hugged each other.

John moved to his mother's side and hugged her to him. Diviña felt small and frail in his grasp. "I wish you would come with us, Mam," he implored through eyes that were misty.

"I'm too old for this adventure and would only slow you down," she laughed. "Take care of the lass, son," his mother whispered, "I entrust her into your hands.

"First, there is nothing old about you, but I will honor your wishes, Mam," he answered solemnly. "Until we're together again...." John's voice trailed off.

Chapter 12 ~ June 1848 - The Road to Dublin

John rode in front, and Tara sat behind. Bailey did not like the knapsack that Diviña had made for him, and fussed for about an hour until the rocking motion of the horse lulled him to sleep. The travelers made good time. Tara had never ridden on a horse and after two hours in the saddle decided that she hated horses. The muscles in her back trembled and her bottom ached. John had been quiet for most of the ride, so she graciously left him to his thoughts. He plodded on throughout the night with no sign that he was planning to take a break. She would dearly love to stretch her sore legs, but was determined that she would not burden him with her troubles by letting him know that she was uncomfortable. It was still dark when they came to a small village John identified as Carrickmacross. There were no signs of life in the tranquil village and the pair continued on. Finally, exhaustion overtook the lass, and she fell asleep using John's back for a pillow. She was shaken from her slumber by the sound of his voice calling her name, and when she opened her eyes she could see that the night had ebbed to dawn.

"There's a secluded meadow and stream just over the rise, and we'll make camp there to rest," said John. "I'm sorry that I didn't stop to let you stretch your legs, but it just would have made it that much harder to remount the horse. It was better to keep going."

"I understand," uttered Tara. Bailey grew restless at the sound of her voice, and all three were happy to arrive at their destination and would be able to get off the horse. John removed the knapsack from Tara's back and set Bailey free to explore the area. He helped Tara dismount. When she tried to stand, the muscles in her legs trembled. As her body began to slump to the ground, John lifted her into his arms and carried her a few paces away from Maggie. He gently set her down on a mound of soft grass and chuckled. "I guess my legs are a wee bit numb," she moaned, somewhat embarrassed. Tara rolled onto her side, and rested her head on the grass so she would not feel any pressure on her backside. The valley was lovely. A small clear stream ran swiftly at its lowest point. Wildflowers grew in profusion all along the edge of the water and up the slope of the glen. Tara wished she could appreciate its beauty, but she was too tired and sore to care.

After John fulfilled the needs of Maggie and set her to graze, he joined Tara on the grass. "Let me look at your cut." he bid. "Mam gave me some medicine and some clean bandages." He looked at the area, and was pleased with what he saw. "Well, I must say, you're a fast healer. This wound is nearly closed. Mam did a fine job with the stitching. She told me I should cut the twine from the stitches in a few days, but we may be able to do it sooner." John busied himself with the contents of his saddle bag. He passed some water over to Tara in a small enamel cup. "Mam said you should drink this birch bark powder that I mixed with water. It'll help ease the aches and pains you must be feeling." Tara gratefully drank the liquid, and the soothing medicine cooled her throat.

"We'll rest here most of the day, and head out again when it gets dark. There'll be less chance of running into anyone who might be looking for a lass of your description," reasoned John. He passed her some bread and cheese. The nutty flavor of the cheese lifted Tara's spirits. Bailey made his way to where they ate, and sat waiting for a handout. "I have something special for you, boy." John reached into his bag and pulled out a large meaty bone wrapped in newspaper.

"That'll keep him busy for hours," professed Tara. The birch bark powder was beginning to ease the pain in her joints. She stretched out on the grass.

"Let's sleep for awhile," said John. "We still have a long way to go."

Tara made a pillow out of Bailey's knapsack. She adjusted the leather strap on the pouch of her bottle, and fell asleep on the cool grass with it cradled in her arms. The next time she awoke, the sun was high in the sky, and John and Bailey were nowhere to be seen. Tara noticed Maggie grazing down by the stream. She decided to test her legs. The aching stiffness in her muscles had lessened, and she slowly stretched her joints as she strolled to the water to bathe. The day was lovely and warm, so she removed her stockings and shoes, hiked up her skirt, and waded in. The cooling flow of the stream eased her tender calves.

Thirty minutes later she saw John and Bailey walking over the rise. John was amusing himself by juggling four balls. At closer inspection she could see that they were not balls at all, but lovely ripe peaches. He smiled as he twirled the fruit deftly in the air.

"You're up. You were sleeping soundly when I awoke, so I took my little pal here for a walk. As we came through the area last night, I noticed a large estate with an orchard about a mile back, so I thought I'd pick us a treat," explained John. He was clearly in a much better mood than yesterday.

Tara smiled and corrected his statement. "You mean you *stole* us a treat."

John laughed. "We Tinkers have an expression. We don't steal. We just, sometimes find things before people know they're lost." He grinned revealing straight white teeth. "Anyway, there were loads of them on the tree. Many were rotting on the ground, lass. Believe me, they'll never be missed." John winked, and tossed a plump offering to Tara. She shrugged and flashed John a smile. It was hard not to laugh at his blarney. Bailey jumped into her lap as she settled on the grass to eat. The sweet juicy fruit tasted like nectar on her tongue.

After they finished the peaches, Tara looked over at John and confessed, "I'm really sorry that I got you into this mess, John. I know you'd rather be camped with Diviña in Cootehill, but I don't know how I would have gotten this far without the help of your family. I'll try to not be a burden to you."

John looked over at Tara but said nothing for a few moments. "'Tis what Mam wanted, and I am doing this for her. I would do *anything* for her," he added protectively.

"Did your Da pass away? Is that why you're so close to your Ma?" questioned Tara.

"I never knew my folks," John stated as he looked squarely into the eyes of the girl. "Mam found me on the streets of Dublin, and I would be dead if it weren't for her." John spent the next hour telling Tara about his life with Shady Mary and how he came to live with Diviña. He shared stories about their experiences on the road, the places to which they had traveled, and the interesting people they had met. "Jack and Rita are my favorites. We stop and see them every time we're in Dublin for a fair. They have four little ones: Roy, Lynette, Kevin, and Teresa. I can't wait to see them. You'll like them a lot."

Tara shared as well. "Up until the troubles with the potatoes, I had never been more than five miles away from our farm. I was happy though. I never thought there was any other way I would want to live. Things have been turned upside down since the troubles."

John reached into his bag and pulled out his whistle, "I wish I could have brought my fiddle, but there wasn't enough room." He began to play a sweet lullaby that Tara knew from childhood. It seemed odd to hear the beautiful delicate music coming from his large muscular hands. Softly, Tara began to sing the story in rhythm with the lilting notes from the wooden flute. When it was over, John looked at Tara and complimented her. "You have a beautiful voice, lass. Do you like to sing?"

Tara made a furrow in her brow and thought for several seconds, "I used to love to sing all the time, but I cannot remember when I have hummed, or whistled, or sang a tune. It has been a very long time since I have even thought about music. Working for the squire left no time for singing. Tell me more about Danny, John. What did you talk about? Did he give you any news about Shauna?" John shared more details with Tara about his visit with her friend Danny.

At dusk, they mounted Maggie to continue their journey. "We'll take this southeasterly trail over these hills tonight, lass, then rest again out of sight tomorrow. From there, the main road leading south will take us to Dublin."

Danny and Shauna chatted in the stable while Danny fed the horses. "I got word to Father Scanlon last night about Tara. He says he'll try to keep the squire headed in the wrong direction for as long as he can. He was very pleased that she is safe," Danny whispered in soft tones.

"The squire has been in a foul mood over the past few days, with he and his posse riding all over the area like they haven't got anythin' better to do! And the butler is just as bad. They're actin' like a couple of spoiled children who've lost their best toy," Shauna looked over her shoulder and murmured softly. "I'd better get back to the kitchen before Cook misses me."

Before she left, Shauna turned to Danny and teased, "So you'll be walkin' me to Mass on Sunday?"

"I told Father Scanlon that I'd be seeing him, so I guess 'tis committed to the task I am," he said smiling shyly.

"Grand, then I'll be waitin' by the porch for you at eight in the mornin'." Shauna flashed Danny a dimpled smile then turned and ran out the stable door.

Later in the day Chase Dellamort and Nevil sat discussing their next strategy when they heard a knock at the door. "Come in!" the squire bellowed.

Mary and a young lad, whom they had never seen before, entered the morning room. The boy was very nervous. He took off his cap, and tried to smooth back a messy crop of red hair that was in need of a good trimming. He was dressed in raggedy clothes and wore no shoes.

"You had better have a good explanation for bringing this guttersnipe into my house, Mary," growled the squire through clenched teeth.

Mary curtsied and spoke. "The boy has some information regarding the whereabouts of Tara, and I thought you might be wantin' to hear the story from his own mouth."

"Speak boy! What do you know about the girl?" snarled the squire.

The boy clutched the hat in his hand. "W-w-well, 'tis just that I have this j-j-j-job cleaning things at the rectory...you know, St Michael's. I w-w-was in Father Scanlon's office sweepin' the s-s-soot out of the fireplace. I heard the priest talking to a man who came to the rectory door. They was t-t-talkin' 'bout that lass you been lookin' for. Ya know, the one that's p-p-posted in the village…with the r-r-reward and all." The boy was very troubled with the information he was imparting to the squire, and he kept his head down while he was talking. "I c-c-come here to this village with me little sister lookin' for work, and the Father gave me…."

The squire interrupted, "Get on with it, you dolt. We don't care about your sorry tale. Tell us what you know about the girl."

"Perhaps I can explain." interrupted Mary. She smiled at the squire looking like the cat that had just caught a mouse for its master.

"What did this simpleton say to you, Mary?" asked the squire in a weary tone.

"The boy said he overheard a man talking to the priest in the rectory hall about Tara. He said he definitely heard the word Tara, and that she was safe and on her way to Dublin. The man told Father that she was going to try to get on a ship to sail home to her family." Mary added, "I asked the lad if he knew who the man was, but he said he never saw his face, and did not recognize the sound of his voice. The boy said that whilst Father walked the man to the front door, he slipped out the priest's office and left by the kitchen door."

The squire turned to Nevil and hissed, "I knew that priest was in on this. I had a feeling all along that he knew more than he was telling."

Nevil asked the boy, "Do you think the priest knows that you overheard him talking to this man?"

"N-N-No," stuttered the child nervously. "When I was d-d-done with the cleanin'. On my way out, I c-c-collected a few pennies from the cook."

"Thank you for your help," said the squire. He dismissed the boy with a wave of his hand. "You may go now."

The boy stood planted, looking down at a flower woven into the Persian carpet.

"Well?" Dellamort growled, "What in blazes do you want now?"

"He wants the reward sir," offered Mary. "He said he only told on the priest for the money. He said he wants it for himself and his little sister."

Dellamort looked at the waif in disgust. "See to it, Nevil," instructed the squire. Looking directly at the boy, he added, "I want you to take this money and collect your sister. You will leave Cootehill today. Immediately. Do you understand me?"

The boy nodded nervously.

In measured tones the squire added, "In fact, if I were you, I'd take your money and try to get yourselves on a ship to America. That's what *I* would do, if I were you. Have I made myself clear?"

Again, the boy nodded and this time there were tears in his eyes.

"Thank you, Mary," said the squire, "you have been most helpful. There will be an extra bonus for you in your wages."

Smiling smugly, Mary followed Nevil as he escorted the boy to his office.

While Nevil was gone, the squire sat brooding. He pondered his options. The plan he was hatching would, in fact, make no sense to most people. After all, the girl had fulfilled her part of the agreement, and, in truth, had stolen nothing from his estate. In fact, the *prize* had ceased to be about the girl at all. It was true that he hated her family for delaying him from possessing the five acres he had coveted for so many years, but the *game* wasn't about his hatred for Michael Maguire either.

His mentality, illogical as it would appear to most decent people, was merely about winning. The squire had an unnatural addiction to gambling and to the thrill of winning. It was a sickness that engulfed his daily life and controlled his better judgment. It was absurd to want to follow Tara to Dublin, track her down like a fox on a hunt, and drag her back to his estate. But in doing so, the squire would feed his unnatural desire to win. His addiction overtook common sense because, quite frankly, Chase Dellamort could not bear to lose. And Nevil Hawkins was a natural ally in his sick schemes because the butler, plain and simple, was just mean. He took pleasure watching others suffer, and he took the most delicious pleasure when they suffered at his own hand.

When Nevil returned he asked, "What are you planning to do, sir?"

Chapter 13 ~ June 1848 - The Road to Dublin

The road to Dublin was wide and well worn, and the pair made good progress. Even though it was night, there were quite a few people heading south. No one paid attention to the two travelers riding double on a horse. They passed several tired looking families pulling handcarts, packed with suitcases and other household belongings into Dublin, presumably to board a ship to North America. Tara's tender muscles ached from all the hours in the saddle, but she did not notice the soreness as much. John took her mind off the pain by amusing her with stories about his life as a Tinker. They passed through the town of Drogheda around midnight. John said they were getting closer to the Irish Sea because he could smell the misty spray of salt in the air. He predicted that Tara might get her first glimpse of the ocean when they reached the seaside town of Balbriggan. He told her that just fifteen miles west of Balbriggan was the famed Tara Hill.

"In 1843, on holy *Lady Day* in August," said John, "our troupe traveled to Tara Hill to hear the great civil rights leader, Daniel O'Connell, speak at a Monster rally. There were more Irish people gathered there than I ever could have imagined. I was only twelve, but I'll never forget the towering great man and his way with the words. When he raised his voice to speak, there was a hush over the crowd. The man's inspiring speech for the future of Ireland rallied the Irish together and gave us pride in our country, and pride in ourselves. He did the best he could for Ireland. There may never be another like him," said John in reverent tones.

Tara had cried at Mass in May when Father Scanlon told his parishioners that their great civil rights leader, Daniel O'Connell, had died peacefully in his sleep while on a pilgrimage to Rome. Father explained that O'Connell's heart had been enshrined in a silver urn that rested in Rome, but his body was coming home on a funeral ship to be buried in Ireland. The land he had held so dear.

Just outside Balbriggan, John stopped at a stream to give Maggie a chance to drink and rest a bit. It was too dark to see the waters of the Irish Sea, but Tara could smell the salty mist of the ocean air, and she could hear the thunderous crashing of the waves as they pounded against the rocky cliffs. "'Tis a powerful mighty sound the sea summons to my ear," she said with awe. "'Tis like the roar of a dragon breathing fire from its nostrils." John laughed as they stretched their legs and shared the last bit of the bread and cheese before traveling again.

When the pair passed safely through Balbriggan, John decided it would be wise to walk on foot to stretch their legs. "It'll give Maggie a rest, and Bailey the chance to run about." Tara was more than happy to oblige. They walked for about an hour until the darkness of night faded to the promise of a new day. The travelers stopped at a small bluff near Skerries, and Tara stared into the eastern horizon as patchy sections of mist parted to reveal the largest body of water she had ever seen.

"'Tis so vast. No wonder so many songs have been written to honor its beauty," she whispered in awe. "The wondrous miracles the Lord has made for us will never cease to astonish me."

"You may think differently about it after you have been sailing on the ocean for a few weeks," said John with a chuckle. "How are you feeling, Tara? Would you like to stop and rest or shall we continue on?"

"In truth, I feel better now that I have been able to exercise my legs. 'Tis a mystery to me how people can ride those things," she said pointing to the horse.

John laughed. "'Tis like anything else, you build up a tolerance for it and in time it doesn't hurt at all. We've made very good time, lass. I know of a clean inn up the road in a village called Swords. I think we should stop for a bite to eat and a pot of tea. If you still feel up to it, we can continue, 'tis an easy ride into Dublin. We could be at Jack's inn before noon."

"I could walk 'til sundown if strengthened with a hot cup of tea," Tara confessed.

John looked at her and said, "You know, lass, I believe you could."

The village of Swords rested near a beautiful little fishing cove. John left Maggie in the capable hands of a stable boy who said he would water and feed the horse while they ate. The small rustic inn was almost empty. A few old fishermen drank tea and chatted quietly in the corner.

John ordered a pot of tea, some bread, and fried codfish. The kind innkeeper brought Bailey some scraps with their food. The tired little dog ate and fell asleep at their feet. Tara thought the tender white flesh of the freshly caught fish tasted wonderful.

"This is the first time I've ever eaten in an establishment such as this. 'Tis too much to take in all in one day," she proclaimed.

"Wait until you see Dublin, lass. 'Tis an amazing city," he stated.

Shauna and Danny watched the dust fly up from the road as Chase and Nevil rode off the estate in the squire's best traveling coach. Danny turned to Shauna and spoke. "As soon as they are out of sight, we must scurry to the Tinkers' camp and warn them that John and Tara are in serious danger. I stopped by their camp last night. They are planning to break camp today and make their way south to Dublin. Let's hope we're not too late. Are you sure you want to do this, Shauna?"

"I've never been more certain of anything in my life, Danny. My things are packed. I hid them in the tool shed. I'm ready to leave this miserable place forever. There's just one more wee thing I need to take care of in the kitchen. Please take my bag, with your things, and wait for me by the road outside the estate. I'll be there soon." Shauna's dimpled smile flashed, hinting at just the wee bit of devilment in her eyes. "'Twill only take a moment," she winked.

Dellamort Manor had been in an uproar all morning. Bags were hastily packed, and Cook, Shauna, and Mary had been instructed to fill a basket with food and other provisions for traveling.

Shauna walked into the kitchen where Mrs. Larkin and Mary stood around the table cleaning up the mess from the provisions for traveling. Mary couldn't wait to gloat.

"The squire was so *pleased* with the information that I uncovered from that stuttering little street urchin, he is rewarding me with an extra bonus in my wages. That little thieving worm will be dragged back to the estate by her hair," Mary proclaimed righteously.

Shauna looked at Mary with loathing. "'Tis just a little confused I am, Mary, as to what you saw Tara steal. Where, again, did all this take place?" asked Shauna in a confused tone of voice.

"'Tis like I told you this morning, Shauna," Mary began in an exasperated tone, "I was coming out of the butler's office a few days ago when I sees her nick the silver vase that's embossed with grapes and ivy. You know, the one that sits on the hall table. She places it in a cloth bag and looks over her shoulder, all suspicious like, and makes her way toward the kitchen door."

"I am still a little unclear, Mary. Are you certain that she took the *grape and ivy* vase?" questioned Shauna innocently.

"Of course, 'twas the grape and ivy vase, you dolt. I'm not an idiot. I know what I saw!"

"'Tis just that I was cleaning the butler's office a while ago, and the oddest thing happened. I found the grape and ivy vase wrapped in a woolen blanket and stuffed behind a chair," said Shauna as she pulled the vase from under the large kitchen table.

Mary was so shocked to be caught in her lie that she opened her mouth to speak, but nothing would come out. She looked like a baby bird waiting for a worm from its mother. At length, she shut the hole closed as her cheeks turned a bright color of crimson red.

Mrs. Larkin gave Mary the sternest of looks before speaking, "Cat got your tongue all of a sudden, has it? I must say, I never much cared for the way you and the butler were always talkin' in whispers. Birds of a feather, I always say. And you, struttin' around this house, as cool as a cucumber. Well mark my words, I'll leave no stone unturned until I get to the bottom of this! That poor sweet child. Quiet as a mouse our wee Tara was, and as good as gold," she sighed. "Mary Tully, get out of my sight. You and Nevil Hawkins make my blood boil!"

By the time Shauna and Danny reached the Tinkers' camp, they were sorely out of breath from laughing and running. The troupe had just finished packing and was beginning to head south. Danny quickly explained to Diviña and the others the squire's plan to try and find Tara in Dublin and kidnap her back to the estate. The Tinkers were pleased to include two more passengers in their travels to Jack Harte's inn in Dublin. Danny and Shauna breathed a sigh of relief, and gratefully watched as the trees of Dellamort Wood faded out of sight from the window of Diviña's caravan

Chapter 14 ~ June 1848 - Dublin

When Jack saw John and Tara standing at the doorway of his inn, he walked over to where the young man stood and hoisted him off the ground like he weighed no more than a barrel of stout. "Jack," proclaimed John, "I'm six foot two and weigh sixteen stone. Put me down, man, or you'll break your back!"

"I will admit, you've grown a fair piece since I saw you last, lad, but not too big for the likes of me," roared the massive man with laughter. "Where's my lovely Diviña?" asked Jack as he looked outside the door, "And who is this pretty lass standing off to the side, all shy?"

Tara instantly fell in love with the mountain of a man with the gentle soul called Jack Harte. He and his wife, Rita, suited each other perfectly, and their children were lively but well mannered. Roy and Lynette clambered all over John while the little ones, Kevin and Teresa, stayed back and timidly looked at the little dog that had come over to be petted.

It took the better part of the afternoon to explain all that had happened to John and Tara in the last few days. Over a pot of tea and cold meat sandwiches, the friends took turns catching up on the events that had happened since they had seen each other last.

"Well I must say, you were incredibly brave to walk off that estate like you did, Tara," remarked Jack. "And it was indeed lucky that our friend John found you in the woods. Things sometimes have a way of working out if it's meant to be," he added smiling across the table at Rita. Jack told them that they could not have had better timing in their arrival.

"My good friend, Captain Joshua Scott, brought a shipment of lumber to Dublin a fortnight ago, and is planning on heading west to New Brunswick in a few days."

"Why does he bring lumber to Ireland?" asked Tara.

"Over the years, most of Ireland's forests have been cut down and shipped to England and other parts of Europe. Lumber is needed for building in Ireland, and it's cheaper to import the stuff from North America than buying it in Europe. It's a fraction of the cost of European lumber, even with the extra distance in shipping costs. Josh is a good captain. His ship, the *Lisa Renee*, is fast and not too bulky. He comes east with a pretty full load, but sailing home his cargo is on the light side. Lots of ships take immigrants on the return trip, but Josh has seen the horrible conditions that a lot of these sea captains have set up. He says they don't care about the passengers, but just do it for the money. Josh is too honorable to mess with any of that. He'll be in later tonight. He loves Rita's cooking, and tonight she's serving roast lamb with mint sauce, and roasted potatoes." Jack Harte's sad account of Ireland's trees made Tara think about Dellamort Wood, and its beautiful trees that had given her so much joy.

Dublin had been a wondrous sight to Tara. The capital city was like a forest of tall buildings. John had pointed out an elegant building called the Custom House, on the quay, so visible in the distance towering near the masts of the ships in the crowded harbor. A procession of immigrants lined the cobblestone road from that majestic building all the way to the harbor. She had never seen anything like it.

The newly laid out streets and squares of Dublin were lined with large Georgian mansions and grand elegant townhouses with brightly painted doors. The city was alive with people on the go. Everything moved so fast. The horses, carriages, and street vendors calling out to sell their wares, added to a level of noise that rivaled the roar of the ocean Tara had heard. Teeming swarms of immigrants were camped by the sides of the docks waiting to be called on board a ship that would carry them to a new life. She was glad that John had suggested they ride into town on Maggie. She felt safer than walking on the crowded streets of Dublin.

Rita showed Tara to an upstairs guestroom. It was very small but clean, and she was happy to have a bed to sleep in. "We don't rent out the rooms anymore. As our family grew, we just didn't have the space. I keep this room for my mother when she comes to visit her grandchildren. John will sleep with the boys in their room. Jack and I make a fine living with the pub downstairs. With so many people coming into Dublin these days, business has never been better."

"I can't thank you enough, Rita. You've been so kind to us," said Tara as she unpacked her satchel and set the bottle next to her bed.

"Jack and I would do anything for Diviña and John. Why, they're like family. Did John tell you that Jack and I met at a fair in Dublin where I was selling cloth in one of the stalls?"

"Yes, he did, and 'tis clear from the way you look at each other, that it was your destiny to meet and fall in love," Tara murmured. "Rita, I hope you'll come to think of me as family, too. I want to help with everything while I'm here."

"That would be grand, Tara. By the way, that's a beautiful green bottle. Diviña has a bottle similar to it, but her bottle is a lovely shade of sapphire blue." Tara smiled as Rita added, "When you've freshened up, come to the kitchen and we'll finish preparing the food for our supper customers."

Later that evening, Captain Joshua Scott said he would agree to take John and Tara on to the Americas, as a favor to his old friend Jack. Captain Scott had a commanding presence about him, and everyone in the pub gathered near to listen as he told a story or relayed a funny incident he had encountered in his travels. The captain had sandy brown hair and bright blue eyes. He was about six feet tall with an athletic build, and had the largest forearms Tara had ever seen. Josh was handsome, and possessed a keen wit to match his easy smile. Something about his presence told Tara, that for all his easy-going manners, he was a man used to giving orders, and would take no nonsense from anyone who tried to cross him. He told John and Tara that he was thirty-two-years-old and had a beautiful wife and three handsome sons. "I'm married to the prettiest little Italian princess in New Brunswick. I can't wait to get home to see her and the lads. My ship is named in her honor," he added with pride, the "*Lisa Renee.*"

Tara could not believe that her ordeal was nearly over. *In three days*, she thought, *I will be sailing home to my family.*

The squire and Nevil were in a foul mood by the time they had reached Dublin. They had pushed hard and were tired when they checked into a hotel near the King's Inn—the renowned gray-stone structure built by the famed London architect James Gandon in 1781.

"What I need is a hot bath and some dinner," Chase said growling at his butler. "Tomorrow we'll comb the port to see if she is registered to sail on one of the ships docked in the harbor. I'll triumph in this quest, Nevil. I swear, that girl will not leave this country, and when I drag her back to my estate she'll be sorry that she ever thought she could outwit me." He sneered angrily at his butler.

The pair spent the next two days searching every passenger list and looking into the faces of melancholy paupers waiting on the docks to leave their homeland forever. "She has to be here somewhere!" Dellamort held a handkerchief to his nose as he and Nevil walked among the throngs of immigrants cooking meals on open fires, washing tattered clothes, and watching barefooted children playing together on the docks. "Look at the way these foul people live. It disgusts me to even look at them," he added disdainfully.

"Perhaps we should check in town again, sir, to see if she has found employment in one of the shops or inns," suggested Nevil. Chase told Nevil he couldn't wait to leave the hoards of filthy peasants at the dock.

Tara almost stumbled when Danny, Shauna, and Diviña came up to the door of Jack's pub the day before she was to leave on Captain Scott's ship. She had been sweeping the floor near the entrance after the lunch crowd had thinned out, and thought she was seeing a mirage. It wasn't until Shauna smiled that Tara knew it was truly she. No one else could possess the same lovely dimples and radiant smile. The girls hugged, and laughed, and cried. "'Tis a miracle, I thought that I would never see you again," sighed Tara.

Introductions were made over tea, and Shauna and Danny relayed the awful incidents that had transpired at the estate. "You're in grave danger, Tara. Those two bullies are hunting for you in Dublin," said Danny.

"You must be very careful, and stay out of sight until you are safely on board the ship tomorrow," added Diviña.

"I don't understand any of this," declared Tara. "Why would they hunt me so? It makes no sense. I've done nothing to them."

Diviña shared, "Sometimes people do evil things which are not understood by those who are good and kind by nature." She shook her head sadly, "There is no sound reasoning behind their actions," she sighed.

"What are you going to do?" asked John to Danny and Shauna. "You gave up your jobs on the estate."

"We were hoping to try and find work in Dublin to save enough money to go to North America," said Shauna.

Jack spoke up, "If you want to go to North America, I think I can persuade my friend, Captain Scott, to find room on his ship for two more passengers. I'll talk to him tonight when he comes in for his supper."

That would release you from your duty," said Tara looking directly at John. With Shauna and Danny sailing with me, I feel certain that we can make it safely to my family. You've done so much already bringing me this far. I can never begin to thank you, John."

John looked at Tara for a moment. Slowly he nodded his head but did not say anything.

"Let me look at your cut," expressed Diviña. "Your wound is nearly healed. You did a fine job removing the stitches, son." After a few moments, Diviña stood up. "Walk me back to our camp, John. I must get back to tell the others that you're safe. We'll see the rest of you back here tonight. I can't wait to meet this captain friend of yours, Jack."

Nevil had been looking in various shops and inns when he caught sight of Shauna and Danny standing at the door of Jack Harte's pub. He licked his lips and smiled when he saw the Tinker woman, hugging Tara. Quickly, he ducked into the doorway of a hat shop until the trio made their way inside. He crept away like a rat to tell the squire of his good fortune.

"You've done well, Nevil," said the squire. "Let's see what the little wench is planning to do!"

The squire paid a spy a few shillings to spend the evening at the pub drinking stout, and eavesdropping on any plans the girl and her friends might be making. Later, the man informed the pair that Tara would depart the next afternoon on a sailing brig called the *Lisa Renee*. In fact, the informer disclosed that the two others, called Danny and Shauna, would be sailing on the ship with her. A look of fury raged across the squire's face, and the spy thought the gentleman's right eye flared an odd shade of ochre. He became anxious to get his money and get away.

The squire was in a calmer mood after he paid the spy, with a warning to keep quiet. He cheered up even more as he and Nevil conspired to come up with the best plan to intercept Tara before she could board the ship. "It's so crowded down by the docks," said Chase to Nevil as the butler packed their things to be ready to leave in the morning. "I feel confident that we can snatch her into my carriage if we're inventive. What we need to find you, Nevil, is a clever disguise." The squire's mood brightened further as he refined the wicked plan he was hatching in his mind. In the end, he felt certain that their devious little scheme was sure to win.

Chapter 15 ~ June 1848 - The Docks

Jack closed the pub to his customers in the morning. He and Rita had risen early to prepared a feast for their friends. Everyone gathered at the tables for a farewell breakfast to fortify the young travelers and bid them goodbye before boarding Josh's ship, which was set to sail with the afternoon tide. Tara could not understand the emotions she was feeling. She was happy that the voyage would bring her home to her family, but she was sad for reasons she could not explain. Her scientific mind tried to rationalize what was bothering her. She thought it must be exactly how her parents felt, knowing they would never see their homeland again.

Captain Scott had agreed to add Danny and Shauna as passengers on board his schooner. Tara had worried that he might not want the added burden of Bailey, but Josh had only laughed. "I always carry fresh livestock such as cattle, hogs, sheep and chickens on my voyages, Tara, so *that* little pup won't upset anything. I sense the comfort your dog must have brought you during this past year of separation from your family, and from the way John tells it, Bailey saved your life. It wouldn't be right if he didn't come along."

Tara looked across the table at John who had been extremely quiet all morning. He smiled at her and shrugged his shoulders.

When the farewell breakfast came to an end, Jack and Rita said their good-byes at the door of the inn. They needed to reopen the pub for the afternoon lunch trade. "If I were a young man, I might consider an adventure on the open seas...carving out a new life in a fresh new land. But I have carved out a good life for me here with my darlin' bride," said a beaming Jack as he gently pulled Rita closer to him.

"Thank you again," said Tara through eyes filled with tears. "I'll write to you the moment I get to Prince Edward Island."

There were hugs and more tears, and Diviña told their friends that she and John would stop back later to share a meal with the family and relate how everything went at the sailing of the *Lisa Renee*. The rest of the Tinkers said goodbye and made their way back to their camp as the others walked in the direction of the dock. Diviña had instructed John to bring Maggie along to carry the bulk of the baggage. Danny offered to hold Bailey so that the throngs of people would not trample him, and Tara carried her bottle strapped across her shoulder and under her arm for safety.

The docks were very crowded. Tara was relieved that she would not have to go in steerage like her family and the many other weary immigrants she saw waiting with wide-eyed apprehension of the trip that lay before them. Still she could not get used to the masses of people surrounding her, marching like determined ants to various destinations. She fell a few paces behind the others. Out of the corner of her eye, Tara saw an old man drop a bundle of turnips he was, obviously, trying to sell to the immigrants. He was dressed in raggedy old clothes. A floppy hat, pulled low over his face, covered his long gray hair. It never occurred to Tara to do anything but stop and help the poor old fellow who was clearly trying to eke out a living selling produce to the people on the docks. She stooped to the ground and began to help the man gather up the scattered turnips. All of a sudden, everything went black as a cloth-sack smothered her bent head. Tara stiffened in terror. A swift hand roughly covered her mouth to muffle the scream that lay buried in her throat.

The sneak attack was quick and had been viciously well planned. No one paid attention as two thugs, hired that morning, swiftly loaded Tara into the squire's carriage parked a few paces from the confrontation. The pair darted away and quickly blended into the crowd. The kidnapping took less than one minute. Nevil casually strolled over to the coach and climbed up front with the driver who cracked his whip in the air to motivate the two horses to move. He hastily removed his hat and gray wig as the horses plodded through the crowded streets in the direction of the road which would lead them north and out of Dublin. It all happened so fast that when John turned to make a comment to Tara, he was shocked to discover that she had vanished into thin air.

The squire ripped the cloth-sack off Tara's head, and sniggered at the stupidity of her kind gesture. His eyes darted in all directions, and the odd color of his right eye caused Tara to gasp in horror. The squire's lips twitched as he sneered into her face. "No one makes a fool out of Chase Dellamort! And no one, especially a Maguire, *wins* but me!"

"Why are you doing this to me?" Tara cried out in anguish. "I've never done anything to you but work hard to provide food for your estate."

"This is not about *you*. This has nothing to do with you, foolish child." His eyes bore into Tara's face as he continued. "I wagered a bet with myself that I could keep you in service for free, but somehow you found out about it. I'll not be made a fool of by a mere child, and I do not like losing!" the squire jeered. "Therefore, you will come back with me, and you will work on my estate until *I say* you can go. You've cause me quite a bit of grief, my dear, and you will be made to pay for it."

Tara had never been more frightened in her entire life. She struggled to fight off the panic gripping her chest, making it difficult to breathe. Frantically, she looked for a way to escape. The muscles in her face trembled as she forced herself to think. Anticipating her dilemma, the squire quickly pulled a thin leather strap from his pocket and tied her hands together. He then tore the scarf from around his neck and gagged her mouth so that she would not be able to cry out.

The actions calmed the squire a bit, and he settled more comfortably into his seat as the carriage meandered slowly through the multitude of people milling about the docks. Suddenly, he noticed the leather pouch strapped over her shoulder and resting at her right side. "What do we have here?" he questioned out loud to himself. Squire Dellamort loosened the top of the pouch and pulled the bottle from its case.

The squire's forehead twitched slightly as his curious eyes opened wide. The man stared at the vessel in his hands for a few seconds before gasping, "What is this mad joke? Are you out of your mind? Why would you choose to carry something as disgusting as this with you?" The tendons in his neck stretched as he choked in exasperated tones. "This...bottle," he hissed, "it is so dark and ugly. I've never seen anything so...hideous in all my life." Although the bottle repulsed the squire, he could not pull his eyes away from the terrible vision before him. "The icy cold touch of this bottle numbs my fingers...and my chest hurts as though a freezing wind is constricting my heart," he said in a voice choked with fear.

Tara looked on in shock. Clearly, the squire was having difficulty breathing. The muscles in the squire's face contorted with pain and revulsion. It took all his energy to tear his eyes from the spell of the bewitching vessel. In a violent gesture, he threw the bottle on the carriage floor and clutched his chest. At that very instant, one of the wheels of the carriage gave way and the coach skidded to a jolting stop.

The jarring motion of the crash brought the squire back to the present moment. He sat in dazed confusion for a few moments gathering strength. "What's the matter now?" he screamed hysterically out the window. The driver and Nevil shouted that the cog pin had come loose on the right rear wheel. In a rage, the squire charged out the carriage door to investigate the problem.

It took Tara a few minutes to recover from the bizarre outburst that had just taken place in front of her. She looked at the floor of the carriage and saw the beautiful emerald green bottle shining up at her. Drawn to its radiance, she reached down and gathered the bottle lovingly into her shackled hands. The minute she did so, the leather strap mysteriously loosened from her wrists and her hands were free. Tara pulled the gag from her mouth and listened. The driver had retrieved the loose wheel and cog pin, and the three men were enlisting help from curious onlookers to reattach the wheel to its axle. Tara knew that this would be her only chance to escape. The squire seemed to have momentarily forgotten about her as he surveyed the liberated wheel. With the bottle still in her grasp, she reached quietly for the handle and slowly opened the door to her left. Quietly, she exited her temporary prison, slipped onto the road, and raced in the direction of the dock.

Tara had always been a fast runner, and she was twenty yards down the road before the squire and the butler began to chase after her. Swiftly, she threaded her way through the hordes of people crowding the thoroughfare leading to the docks. Tara dared not look over her shoulder for fear that the gesture would slow her down.

A worried John had instructed the others to get to the *Lisa Renee* where they might have a better view of the dock while he frantically searched through the crowd to find Tara. His height gave him the advantage of seeing over most of the people milling about the dock, and the muscles in his neck strained as he frantically looked for Tara among the swarming throng of people. A flash of green light, reflecting off the sun, caught his eye, and he was thrilled to see Tara running in the direction of the ship. The squire and the butler pursued her from twenty paces back. The two men screamed hysterically for people to grab her, but the level of noise among the crowd muffled the frantic cries of the well-dressed gentlemen.

"Tara," yelled John, "I'm over here!" John continued to shout and wave his arms until he caught her attention.

Tara saw her tall friend, waving wildly over the heads of the crowd thirty yards ahead, and gratefully raced to where he was making his way toward her. "Thank God, you're here," she sobbed as she toppled into the safety of his grasp. Together, they turned to race up the walk that led to the ramp of the *Lisa Renee*. Diviña, Shauna, and Danny were overjoyed when they saw the pair rush up the gangplank and onto the deck of the ship.

Captain Joshua Scott had been overseeing the last minute rigging of the sails with his men when he heard the commotion. He was always a little nervous before any voyage and was not happy with the disturbance that was taking place on the deck of his ship. By the time he reached the area near the gangplank, he was not in good spirits.

Squire Chase Dellamort and Nevil Hawkins had followed John and Tara onto the deck of the ship and were heatedly arguing with the group of friends. Several curious people had gathered at the bottom of the ramp and were watching the quarrel take place above them. John placed Tara protectively behind him while Danny stepped next to John to fortify the barrier.

"What's the meaning of this?" challenged Captain Scott, as he walked up to the group.

Smiling, Chase Dellamort walked over to Josh and extended a gloved hand with the air of an aristocrat. Joshua, who was in no mood for formalities, barked, "You, sir, have not been invited aboard my ship, so state your business." He added, "This interruption better be justified. I do not like to be called away from my duties when I am preparing my brig to sail."

"This will not take much of your time, Captain," said the squire in a genteel tone of voice. "This girl," he announced, pointing to Tara, "was an employee at my estate until last week. She stole some valuable silver from me and escaped in the night. Acting on a tip, my butler and I tracked her to Dublin. I want you to hand her over to me, so that she may be brought north to Cootehill and prosecuted for her crime," the squire declared with authority, "Captain, I can see that you're a busy man. Do not bother yourself with this tedious affair. Hand her over to me, and I will see that justice is served." The squire took a step forward toward Tara.

Tara was stricken with apprehension listening to the smooth reasoning behind the squire's lies. *I've come so far, and now I'll be taken away for sure.* Without even knowing that she was doing it, Tara began to pray to Granny Cassie for help.

"You lie, sir!" asserted Shauna in a firm voice that expressed outrage. She turned to the captain and implored. "Do not believe the deception that this man speaks with easy practice. Tara was betrayed by the cunning of these two men so that the squire wouldn't have to fulfill his agreement to pay her passage home after she completed a year of service working for him." "The day I left his estate, I found the *very* silver they accused her of stealing in the butler's office, and I caught their accomplice, another servant named Mary, in a lie. The supposedly stolen silver now rests in the possession of Mrs. Larkin, the cook."

The captain noticed that the butler's face twitched slightly as Shauna shared this last bit of information. Captain Scott turned to Tara and asked, "Did you steal from this man's estate?"

Through years of dealing with the many sailors who comprised his crews, Joshua Scott had learned to get to the heart of a problem, read a situation correctly, and deal with it swiftly and decisively. He studied the character of the young girl who stood before him and took in every word that she articulated. He paid particular attention to her eyes.

With the Emerald Bottle still clutched in her hands, Tara drew in a breath of air, stepped around John and Danny and faced the captain squarely, "Captain Scott, I worked for one year under the cruel dominance of these two men. 'Twas the hardest work that I've ever done in my life. I did my best to honor my family and fulfill the agreement made by my father in writing and signed in the squire's hand. In the last days of my service, I overheard them plotting to falsely accuse me of this crime while I tended some roses planted under an open window. They were laughing that their plan would keep me in servitude to them for several more years. In that moment, I knew that all was lost to me, so I left Dellamort Estate that night. I took nothing with me but the hope that I might find a way to be free from their tyranny and make my way home to my family. I stole nothing from this man, Captain, and I'll swear to it if that is your wish."

Captain Scott looked at Tara for about ten seconds. He nodded once and slowly turned to Squire Dellamort. "I believe the words of this young woman, and I order you to leave my ship immediately."

"Surely, Captain, you cannot be serious. Do you know who I am?" voice the arrogant squire.

When the captain did not speak, the squire answered his own question. "I happen to be Squire Chase Dellamort of Dellamort Estate, and I will not be treated like a common..."

"You may be a pretentious tyrant in your own petty kingdom but this is *my* domain, your *lordship*, and when an order states *immediately*, it means just that." Captain Scott nodded at John and smiled. In one swift movement, Josh closed in on the squire and grabbed him, with one hand, by the seat of his pants, while the other hand clutched his coat collar with the grip of a vice. The veins in Josh's powerful forearms bulged as he hoisted the small man up on his toes and escorted him down the gangplank. The petrified butler tried to dart out of harm's way but John was too quick, and taking his lead from the captain, marched the butler in the same direction.

For most of the immigrants, the ordeal of waiting to be processed to sail out of Ireland was a monotonous and tiresome experience. Therefore, the scene on the *Lisa Renee* created an amusing diversion, in the long dull afternoon for the large crowd that had gathered to witness the disagreement in progress, and they watched with considerable merriment. The assemblage listened to the lively discussion on the *Lisa Renee* with the enthusiasm of an audience who might have paid to see an elaborate Shakespearean drama.

An old Irish fisherman, carrying a very large basket of freshly caught sardines to market, had been one of the first on the scene to enjoy the controversy. He stood near the bottom of the ramp as the captain and the tall youth ungraciously escorted the two dandies off the ship. Half way down the plank the men were given a hardy shove, and the pair struggled to keep their balance as they tottered to the bottom of the ramp.

Now it sometimes happens when a large group forms, that people will bear witness with varying reflections. Later, some said the squire and the butler ran into the fishermen and that caused the mishap. Others swore that the old man purposely dropped his basket, scattering the fish directly in the path of the two men moments before the blunder. Only the fisherman could be certain as to what had truly happened, and he remained elusively silent over the controversy.

Just as the two men were beginning to recover their balance after their rather hasty and undignified escort down the ramp, they skidded on the collection of the smelly slick sardines and toppled unceremoniously onto their backsides. As the two writhed in the smelly slime, each tried to stand grabbing the other to steady his motion. This only complicated an already shaky predicament, and merely added to the mess and mayhem. A thunderous explosion of laughter discharged from the throngs of the immigrants who were witnesses to the amusing spectacle.

"Let go of me, you nincompoop!" screamed the squire to his butler. Realizing that he would get no assistance from Nevil, Squire Dellamort crawled like an infant on his hands and knees until he was outside the circle of muck. The unkempt squire wiped his hands on his coat and stood glaring at the guffawing crowd. Nevil eventually managed to regain his footing, and the disheveled pair stood together to face their delighted audience.

The squire glanced briefly at the men staring down at them from the ship and shuddered. Trying to muster a last shred of dignity, he turned to Nevil and announced, "Let us go now, Nevil, and remove our selves from these uncivilized barbarians." The crowd guffawed.

Their wrinkled clothes were covered in slime and coated with shiny silver bits of fish scales. The smell of the sardines had penetrated the fibers of their garments, and had saturated the strands of their hair. As Squire Chase Dellamort and Nevil Hawkins retraced their path back to the carriage, every immigrant huddled at the docks that afternoon retreated in amused horror. The two cut a wide path through the crowd, reminiscent of Moses parting the Red Sea in the Old Testament.

Tara was so happy that she raced over to John and the captain and hugged them both. "That was wonderful! Until my dying day," she exclaimed, "I'll never forget the vision of those two sloshing about amongst those fish. You two have made me the happiest girl in Dublin. I'm forever in your debt."

"I was happy to oblige, Miss Maguire," answered the captain. "I must say, that little diversion did release some of the tension I always feel before a voyage. Tipping his cap, he added, "Please excuse me while I prepare this ship to sail, or we might lose the tide." The captain chuckled again as he walked away from the group.

The friends spent a few minutes reliving the incident until Diviña suggested, "We had better be going, John, so that the captain can make the tide."

John turned to look at his mother but did not move. He was clearly troubled.

"What's the matter, son? Why are you distressed?" asked Diviña.

"Mam, I don't know what to say. I love you so much, but I want to go, too."

"John," said Diviña smiling, "I was wondering when you were finally going to come to terms with the conclusion I had realized a week ago."

"You knew?" John gasped.

"It is my intuition, John, to know what destiny is best for my own son," she smiled reassuringly.

"Come with us Mam," John implored. "Come build a new life with us in a new land," John pleaded, repeating the words of Jack Harte.

"It is *my* destiny to stay in Ireland, son. It is written in the stars." Diviña smiled with shining eyes.

"What'll I do?" groaned John. "All my belongings are back at the camp. I've nothing but the clothes on my back."

"John, I had a fairly strong feeling that you might change your mind at the last minute. Therefore, your uncles and I had your things brought to the ship and stored below last night," Diviña explained.

"But...what if I had decided not to go...my things..." John's voice trailed off.

"I felt fairly certain that you *would* want to sail on this journey...but...just in case...well, why did you think I suggested that we bring Maggie along?" she laughed.

"The captain has allowed me to come too? I do not understand. Why is the captain doing this for us?" John asked, puzzled.

"Joshua and Jack are very old friends, John. I know that Jack once saved the captain's life, although I am not certain of all the details. Captain Scott is allowing you and the others to sail on his ship as a favor to Jack. It will be up to the four of you to prove that you're worthy of this gesture made between two friends. Captain Scott is a sensible young man, but he doesn't tolerate foolishness, as you witnessed a moment ago. He is, however, in a particularly fine mood at the moment, because I read his fortune last night. The captain acted quite skeptical, but in truth, he was thrilled when I told him that his wife is expecting their fourth child...a little girl," Diviña winked.

"Mam, you're the most incredible woman I've ever known, and I promise we'll earn the trust of the captain and make you proud."

"Son, you have always made me proud," she proclaimed.

"Quickly, Danny," requested Diviña, "kindly put your expertise to work and bring Maggie on board, please. Captain Scott has prepared a stable for her with the rest of the livestock."

"Grinning broadly, Danny said, "I will, ma'am." He tipped his cap and dashed down the ramp.

John looked at his mother with a heavy heart. "You've given me everything, Mam. I would be dead if not for you and Jack. Everything that I am…is because of you. How can I bear to leave you now?" he grieved.

"Son, you were in my heart before I found you in Dublin, and you will be in my heart when you leave me now. Time and space can never separate us. The bond of love that we share is woven as tight as a ball of twine." Diviña kissed her son. When she pulled away she looked into his face and smiled with the lively brown eyes that were the window to her soul.

John could not help but smile back at her because at that precise moment in time, the ageless matriarch looked like a young girl. *This is the way I always want to remember you.*

Tara watched the pair from a distance with tears in her eyes. She knew what it felt like to say goodbye to loved ones. Tara was overjoyed that John would join the three friends on their voyage. It was the missing fragment of thread that stitched the journey into place. Slowly, she walked over to them and the three hugged as one.

Chapter 16 ~ July 1848 - The Lisa Renee

Captain Scott shook his head in disbelief every time he thought about it. "I've made more voyages across the Atlantic than I can remember," he said to Bud Ellis, his first mate, "but can you ever recall a voyage as blessed as this, Buddy?"

"Can't say that I 'ave cap'n. This 'ere sailin' voyage h'is most remarkable. The weather 'as been loverly, the wind 'as been up and at a steady pace. Been 'ardly a 'int of trouble. H'if we keep going h'at this stride, h'it will be a record breaking trip for certs," remarked the first mate in a broad Cockney accent.

"When Diviña thanked me for taking the young ones to North America, she told me that the good deeds people do are always rewarded. If this is what she meant, remind me to make a practice of doing more of them in the future, Buddy," said Josh laughing.

"Aye, aye, and h'amen to that cap'n," answered Buddy.

The *Lisa Renee* was seventy-five feet long and twenty-five feet wide. It was built solidly from North American pine and hardwoods in New Brunswick. She had been given a First-Class, Division Three rating and was meticulously cared for by the captain and his crew. The sound slender brig was built in 1838 and proved to be a profitable little laborer for Josh in the ten years he had owned her. Two sturdy masts moored the huge canvas sails that strained against the southwesterly winds that steered the ship toward North America. The ship contained a decent galley, an eating room to accommodate twelve people comfortably, and quarters for the sailors and first mate. The captain's cabin was small but comfortable and efficient. The ship contained an extra cabin for guests, but was often used to store extra supplies. That room was given to the girls since they were the only women on board and needed a measure of privacy.

The full load of lumber the captain brought to Ireland had long since been sold to merchant brokers in Dublin. The bottom hold of the ship was only partially filled with the goods he carried on the return trip to New Brunswick. All in all, it was a profitable little business for Captain Scott, and he very much enjoyed his life sailing to different ports.

After their first week at sea, Tara stood alone near the front of the ship watching the sun set in the western horizon when Captain Scott joined her. "I never tire of seeing the sun sink into the ocean when I'm on a voyage. It's rare, but every so often I witness a flash of light the most brilliant shade of green just as the sun sets into the ocean. I'm baffled as to what causes it."

Tara nodded. "The sunset is indeed a beautiful sight. It almost appears as though the sun is being swallowed by the sea." The two stood watching, and just as the sun dipped its last bit of light, from the orb, into the ocean, a brilliant flash of emerald green exploded on the horizon. Tara and the captain looked at each other and laughed in amazement. At length Tara spoke. "Captain, can you tell me something about the carved wooden figure of the beautiful woman on the prow of the ship? I love her flowing wind-swept hair. She has such a look of contentment."

The captain smiled. "That is my wife, Lisa Renee," he boasted proudly. "I engaged an artist from Nova Scotia to capture her beautiful face. Whenever I'm lonely, I come up to the bow of the ship and talk to her," he said. "The life of a sailor can be solitary at times. I miss my family when I'm at sea," he added wistfully. "I hope Diviña is right about the baby, though I don't put much stock in fortune tellers. I have, however, been longing for a little girl who might look just like her mother."

"Although nothing can be certain in life, Captain, I think you may be surprised and get your wish," encouraged Tara.

"I'm curious about something," said the captain.

"What is it, Captain? Please, feel free to ask me anything."

"What's that little bag you seem to always carry at your side, Miss Maguire?"

Tara removed the bottle from its pouch as she spoke. "This bottle was given as a gift to me by Diviña. It is a special bottle, and I believe it has the ability to help people who are on a journey. Already, it has been most helpful to me."

"What do you mean?"

"Well, for one thing," she smiled, "it brought me to you and your ship which is carrying me on this voyage home."

Captain Scott studied the bottle for a while before he spoke. "It's a pretty enough little bottle, but I can assure you, Miss Maguire, it had nothing to do with me allowing you aboard my ship. You and your friends are here because of a favor I owe to my friend, Jack Harte, and nothing more."

"That may well be true and believe me, Captain Scott, we are most grateful. But the bottle has helped me out of other situations since it's been in my possession. 'Tis difficult to explain, but I have come to appreciate the comfort it's given me."

"If the bottle makes you happy, then who am I to deny you this pleasure, Miss Maguire?"

"Captain, please feel free to call me Tara," she spoke in earnest.

"You must understand, Miss Maguire, this is strictly a business arrangement, and I don't generally make a habit of getting too involved with my passengers." The captain held the girl in his gaze for a moment and said, "We'll see."

It was a lovely July afternoon on their ninth day at sea. Captain Scott's sailing brig cut through the sea like a knife slicing through a ripe melon. It was clear that the first mate, six sailors, and the cook respected the captain very much. So far, the crew and the four passengers had been enjoying each other's company, which made for a harmonious trip. The sun warmed the air with a comfortable breeze, as its rays danced off the ocean swells creating a sparkling profusion of light and color. Its beauty reminded Tara of the luminous colors of the bottle when Diviña had first showed it to her in the caravan. The friends were in high-spirits as they sang to the music of John's fiddle and visited on the rear deck of the ship.

"'Twas gracious of Captain Scott to give us his guest quarters," remarked Shauna in a jovial mood. "I have not had this much peace of mind since I was a wee toddler at Ma's knees. John, it gives me comfort to know that your sweet Diviña will travel to Ballybay to tell Ma that I've sailed to the Americas. Your Ma said she would explain everythin' to her and tell her not to worry. I'll be forever grateful to her for taking me and Danny away from that horrible place," Shauna shuddered.

Tara walked over and put an arm around her friend's shoulder, "We all are, Shauna." At length Tara spoke again. "After Ma's letter, I was very worried that I wouldn't like being on the ocean so far-away from land, but thus far, our journey has been blessed," sighed Tara, "and I've seen enough incredible sights in this past week to last a lifetime."

"Sleeping in a hammock is a lot more comfortable than I first imagined," said John. "The ship starts to rock, and I'm lulled to sleep like the bewitching spell of a fairy." He looked at Tara and laughed. "There's something about this fresh ocean air and sun that snuffs me out like a lamp at night."

"I just hope the good weather lasts," commented Danny. "Have I mentioned that I don't know how to swim?" he added nervously.

"YES!" John, Tara, and Shauna answered in unison.

John and Danny had spent the morning sweeping and swabbing the deck, while Tara and Shauna helped the cook, a handsome young lad named Little Joe, in the galley. The four were so grateful for the chance to sail on Captain Scott's ship that they wanted to help, but without getting in the way of the duties of the sailors.

"John, please play us another tune on your fiddle," requested Tara.

"I'm still amazed that Mam had it brought on board with my other things," sighed John. He picked up the violin and began to play a lively jig. The girls and Danny danced together until two off-duty seamen joined in the fun. A sailor, named Michael McNamara, twirled Tara around the deck while John looked on with a bewildered expression. At length, Michael asked John if he could borrow his fiddle to play a few seafarers tunes. John happily handed over the strings to McNamara and invited Tara to dance to the melody of a little sea-ditty.

The wind held brisk, without throwing too much spray over the sides of the ship. Captain Scott and Buddy wandered over to observe the merriment. Applauding Michael for his efforts on the fiddle, Captain Scott announced, "If the wind holds true, this may be the fastest voyage we've ever made sailing west. I reckon we might make it to New Brunswick in a record time of twenty-seven days," he announced.

"We once made the trip to Dublin h'in twenty-four days, but h'it h'is always a faster trip 'eading h'east because the wind is h'at our backs," added Buddy. "You young'ns 'ave brought considerable luck to this journey," he praised.

"I don't know about luck," said Josh glancing at the bottle strapped at Tara's side, "but I look at other ships sailing near us, and we always seem to catch the best wind and just glide past them. There are things about this trip that seem charmed. I don't ever recall having seen the large number of porpoises swim with us, which is always a good omen."

Tara and the others had thrilled the first time they saw a school of the majestic mammals leaping high out of the water in concert with the movement of the brig. Tara delighted at their playful nature. It was almost as though they enjoyed the company of humans. Over one hundred of the graceful creatures had cruised with them for over an hour. "If I were a mermaid, Bailey," she joked, "I think that I'd definitely have a porpoise for a pet."

It took Bailey a few days to adjust to life at sea, but the smart little dog adapted quickly. Tara took him to the livestock area and taught him to do his business on an area of straw. It took Maggie a little longer to connect with her new surroundings, and John spent long hours reassuring her, in soft tones, that everything was going to be fine. Her appetite picked up after the first three days.

On another day they spied a lone blue whale slowly swimming near the ship. Captain Scott was amazed. "It's very unusual to see a blue whale so far south in July," he shared. "Blue whales usually spend their summers near the icy waters of the polar regions." He told Tara that the female is always larger than the bulls and that a calf will stay with its mother, nursing, for six or seven months. "This female looks to be almost one hundred feet long." It was true that the whale did look to be longer than the ship to Tara. "She must be old and couldn't make the trip north," he calculated. Josh told the youngsters that a blue whale must eat a ton of plankton and krill each day to stay healthy. "I've talked to whalers in New Brunswick who have extracted over eight thousand gallons of oil from just one whale." Tara had watched the whale dive under the water and stay out of sight for twenty minutes before rising to the surface again. The whale further delighted her when it shot a spray of water twenty feet in the air from its spout. When it disappeared again, she lost sight of it for good.

As the passengers and mates enjoyed the music of the fiddle, the cry of a sailor was heard from above. Tara looked up to see the youngest of the crew, Travis Meek, dangling in the ropes of the masts by his left foot. She turned her head away as the boy screamed in pain.

Captain Scott sprang into action. "Quick, Michael, get to the wheel and tell Chad to steady the ship. Buddy, I'm going to need your help to get the lad down. Grab some rope."

"Aye, aye, Cap'n."

Captain Scott and Buddy scaled the ropes of the mast with the ease of two monkeys climbing a tree. They reached the dangling sailor in seconds. "Lie still, Travis, and let us do our job." The boy's faced winced in pain, but was able to nod. "Buddy, we'll lift him onto my back together." The first mate nodded. "Lash him to me with this rope, then you can untangle his foot from the webbing."

"Aye, aye, Cap'n."

The muscles in the captain's forearms bulged as he lifted the lad by the belt of his pants into an upright position. The movement caused the boys to scream out in pain.

From the deck below, Tara watched in horror. She gathered the bottle to her chest without knowing that she had even done so. At that moment, Travis mercifully fainted and fell limp into the captain's arms. This helped Buddy secure the boy to Joshua's back and free his ankle. It flopped at an odd angle, as blood poured from an exposed wound caused by the jagged edge of a broken bone.

Buddy threaded his way to the deck followed by the captain and the still unconscious Travis. They laid him on a blanket that had been brought up from below deck by Danny. "We're going to have to set the bone in his leg, and we best do it while he's out cold," said Josh. "Hold him steady while I pull it into place."

"Please let me help?" asked John. "I have assisted my mother with injuries such as this, and I know how to stitch a wound closed."

The captain looked at John for a brief moment and then nodded.

In the same confident tone Diviña used in emergencies, John directed Danny. "Danny, bring my medical tools from my satchel. You'll find them in a small black leather pouch." Danny nodded and did as he was asked.

Buddy grabbed the boy under his armpits and pulled as the captain strained his muscles to ease the bone back into position. John pushed on the area until he felt the bones were aligned correctly. When they both agreed that it looked set, they slowly released the pulling pressure. Travis never moved during the ordeal.

Soon Danny appeared with the black bag, and John stitched the wound closed using the method his mother taught him while he assisted her with her patients. Captain Scott looked on in silence. The gash was drawn together by the needle into neat rows of twine. John cleaned the blood from the area and wrapped the leg in clean white cotton cloth stored for emergencies such as this.

"You are deft with the needle, John. We're lucky that you are so skilled," said Joshua.

"Thank you, Captain. I believe his wound should heal all right, but what we've got to look for now is an infection. If gangrene sets in, we may have to cut his leg off."

Tara shuddered at the thought.

Buddy brought some scraps of wood from the hold of the ship, and John secured them with strips of cotton cloth to stabilize the broken ankle. They carefully carried Travis to the captain's quarters where he could lie flat on a proper bed. All they could do was wait and see.

Chapter 17 ~ July 1848 - The Lisa Renee

Tara and the others took turns nursing Travis. It was late into the evening on the third day. Tara placed drops of birch bark tea on the lad's lips, but it was hard to make him drink. She had applied all her skills to bring down the swelling in a leg bloated to double its normal size. Sweat saturated a body consumed with fever. Sensing the gravity of the situation, Tara sent for Captain Scott.

"Gangrene is bound to set in. I hate to do it Miss Maguire, but I think that we may have to take his leg," said the captain as he looked at the boy moaning in his bed.

"Please, Captain Scott, let me try one more thing," pleaded Tara.

"What can you do now that we haven't already tried?"

"I have filled my bottle with seawater, and with your permission, I'd like to bathe the wound with it."

"Have you lost your mind? What good would that do?" The anguished captain was losing patience.

"I'm not sure that it will do *anything*, but something is compelling me to try this method of treatment. Please Captain, a young boy's leg is at stake." Tara was unsure what was causing her to insist on the treatment with the bottle, but she felt driven to persist.

"Better to lose a leg than a life!" the captain barked. Tara looked at the captain with an expression of pain. With reluctance, he relented, "I'll give you twenty-four hours. If there's no improvement, the leg *will* come off. Do I make myself clear?"

"Yes. Thank you, Captain Scott."

Tara thought that the captain would get back to his duties, but he surprised her when he stayed to watch her pour small drops of seawater, from the Emerald Bottle, directly over the gash that had been stitched by John. Travis shook once with a jolt, let out a deep sigh, and slipped into an intense level of sleep. The captain shook his head and mumbled as he walked out the door, "I hope to God you know what you're doing, Miss Maguire!"

I hope I know what I'm doing too. Please, Granny Cassie, help me. I do not want this boy to lose his leg, but I don't want him to die because of some foolish notion that I can save his leg.

Tara continued the treatment of ocean water, poured from the bottle, for the remainder of the evening and late into the night. Long after the others had gone to sleep, John appeared with a cup of tea and few biscuits. "Thank you, John." She only picked at the food.

"Why don't you let me take over, lass? You look very tired."

"Shauna already offered, but I can't leave him, John. 'Tis as though his life is tied to mine. I must stay and continue the treatment."

"You'll make yourself sick, if you don't eat and rest. Let me continue the treatment while you rest your head on the captain's desk. What are you doing for him?"

Tara yawned. "I pour the ocean water over his wound from the Emerald Bottle every fifteen minutes. I don't know if 'tis doing any good, but he seems to be resting easier. I think the swelling in his leg is receding, but it *could* be wishful thinking." Tara handed John the bottle and rested her head in her arms. She was asleep in two minutes.

Tara was startled awake by a tap on her shoulder. She looked up to see John standing over her smiling. "How long have I been sleeping? I only meant to nod off for a few minutes."

"Don't fret about that, lass. Come and see your patient."

The ache in her back throbbed as Tara rose to follow John the short distance over to the captain's bed. Streaks of pink and aqua, peeking through the porthole window, signaled that dawn was fast approaching. She yawned and smiled as she looked at her patient. "Travis, 'tis so nice to see that you're feeling better. You gave us all quite a scare." She pulled back the cover to inspect his leg. The swelling had gone down around the area of the stitching and there was less redness. Tara put her hand to the lad's head. His fever had broken.

"We did it, John. I don't know how, but we did it. I'll go and tell the captain and the others." Tara stopped at the door of the cabin and turned around. "Thank you, John," she said as she flashed him a huge smile.

"I did very little. The lad has you to thank for his leg. But if you're feelin' a wee bit beholden' to me, I wouldn't say no to a cup of tea if you felt so inclined."

"I'll bring you the whole pot," she laughed.

When the captain saw the improvement Travis had made, he smiled and shook his head in wonder. "I don't know what just happened here. I've never seen a man come back from an infection such as the one he had. You're a lucky lad, Travis. You owe your leg to Miss Maguire."

"I know, sir, I can never thank her enough for what she's done for me."

"What happened up there on the rigging?" asked Captain Scott.

"It's my fault, sir, and it won't happen again. I was enjoyin' the fiddle music and dancing on the deck when the wind shifted a bit. I wasn't braced as well as I should've been, and I lost my balance. Lucky for me, my foot got hung up in the rigging or I'd be dead for sure."

"A sailor can lose his life on a ship if he doesn't have his wits about him at all times. I've seen it happen, Travis. Hopefully you've learned from this mistake. The second time it happens we might not have Miss Maguire to work her *miracles* on you."

"There won't be a second time, Captain Scott. I promise."

Captain Scott motioned John and Tara to step out the door of his cabin. He looked back into the cabin at Travis. "I took you on board my ship as a favor to Jack, and nothing more, but I want you to know that it is I who have been granted a favor. Thank you for saving that boy's life. I'm not sure I understand everything about this bottle of yours, Miss Maguire, but I don't deny that something unusual has happened over the past few hours." The captain smiled and faced Tara squarely.

"Do you remember our conversation on the prow of the ship our first week at sea?"

"Why yes, Captain, I believe I remember most of it. And in particular, the beautiful green flash of light just as the sun set into the ocean." she cautiously replied.

"Yes that was an amazing sight. You may remember that you asked me to call you Tara, and I said I didn't like to get too involved with my passengers."

"I remember, Captain."

"Well, it would be an honor if the request to call you Tara is still open. And, by the way, my friends call me Josh."

"The invitation to call me Tara has always been open, Captain, and 'twould be an honor to call you Josh."

Travis made remarkable gains over the next few days. He insisted on moving back to his hammock. "You've been without your quarters far too long, Captain. Buddy made me a crutch out of wood scraps, and soon I'll be able to hobble about on that. Thank you, sir, for everything."

"You be careful, Travis. It looks like you'll be able to walk without crutches soon, and Tara wouldn't want you to re-injure yourself after all her hard work nursing you back to health." The good luck with weather and wind continued over the next week as Travis made remarkable progress with his recovery.

On their nineteenth day at sea, the ship's bell sounded and the group knew that the cook was calling them to dinner. Little Joe had made a hearty vegetable and lamb stew from the livestock that the captain carried in the hold of the ship. "You can't expect men to do their best work if they are not fed well, and I was lucky to find a cook as clever as Little Joe," Captain Scott had told his passengers.

Tara was amazed to have fresh milk for her tea, but Little Joe had said, "The captain and his men would rather go to sea without ale than without a milking cow or some nanny-goats. 'Tis my job to keep the cow healthy," he said proudly. "Once when her supply fell off, I fixed to bring her around again with a bountiful ration of Irish stout."

The cook told the girls that pigs were the most useful stock, "Little piggies have good sea legs, and a hearty constitution." The floating farm, which also included chickens and ducks, made Tara wonder what it must have been like for Noah on his ark.

The captain, some of the sailors, and the four passengers were just finishing off their meal with a seed cake and some tea, when one of the night crew rang the signal bell for the captain and crew to come up on deck. After the fine luck they had experienced, Tara said a quick prayer hoping nothing had gone amiss. The four friends hung back to let the crew man their positions. Then, slowly, they climbed up the steps that led to the deck to see if their help was needed.

The sight that lay before them took Tara's breath away. The captain and all of his crew were staring upward, in reverent silence. The masts, the rigging, and the sails of the ship were suffused with a phosphorescent glow like a blue-violet flame. The color illuminated the water around the ship. Everyone on board stared at the mystical sight without uttering a word. At length Captain Scott spoke. "I've read about this, and I have heard other seaman talk about it, but it can't be appreciated until it happens to you."

"What is it, Captain?" asked Tara.

"If it is...what I think it is," said Josh in awe, "this rare display of light is a phenomenon known as St. Elmo's Fire, Tara."

"What is St. Elmo's Fire?" gasped Danny.

"No one really knows what causes it, Danny, but it can happen on a spire of a tall building or church, or it's been known to happen on the top of a mountain. Mostly, I have heard that it happens at sea, and that is how it got its name. You see, St. Elmo is the patron saint of fisherman. Ancient fishermen believed that when a ship became alight with St. Elmo's Fire, it was a sign of protection. This strange light always appears at night in all kinds of weather, even on a calm night such as this. No one knows how or why it happens, but everything lights up in this mysterious way. Then, as quickly as it comes, the light fades away."

It was true that the beautiful luminous color that had caused the rigging to glow was beginning to fade. Every member on board the ship stood and watched until the magical light faded into the night. Josh shook his head. "This is a trip that I'll be telling my grandchildren about when I'm an old man in my rocking chair, for sure," said Josh as he scratched his head and looked at the four travelers standing near him.

The captain reckoned that they were four days away from New Brunswick. He told his passengers that he always manned his ship with extra watchmen when he got this far north to look for icebergs. "The greatest danger occurs in winter, but the spring months also make a ship at risk. "Even in July," he added, "I don't like to sail at night this far north unless there is a full moon and clear skies, like now." He told them that icebergs are formed from huge chunks of fresh-water glaciers from the Arctic, which break off into the sea, and float south with the currents. "I've seen ones that measure a mile long, and as tall as a twenty-story building. The ones we usually see in July are little ones. We call them growlers because they make noise moving in the waves. Any captain, worth his salt, will be extra attentive when they are in iceberg territory."

Danny told the captain about his family's troubles coming to New York on the *Hannah*. "I read about that in the newspaper, Danny. Mr. Shaw and his two mates are cowards, in my opinion. And after all the big summon for justice in the paper, I heard that he was not punished, and that he still sails the seas." Tara looked over at Danny and saw his shoulder's droop when he heard this discouraging information. To Tara, it was disheartening to learn that there had been no justice for Danny's family and the rest of the passengers on the *Hannah*.

A few days later Tara did see a small iceberg, but it was well away from their course and no danger to the ship. She gave a silent thanks to Granny Cassie that their voyage had been so truly blessed.

The *Lisa Renee* sailed up the Bay of Fundy to Saint John in grand style. Tara could see dense forests to her left in New Brunswick and more to her right in Nova Scotia. The forests of pine, oak, birch, maple, and spruce trees made Dellamort Wood seem very small. And just as the captain and Buddy had predicted, the sturdy vessel sailed safely into the harbor of Saint John, New Brunswick on the last day of July 1848. The trip had taken only twenty-seven days. It set a record for the fastest trip west the crew had ever experienced. Captain Scott's wife, Lisa Renee, and his three sons had seen them sail into the harbor from their house above the bay. The couple embraced in the manner of those who have been separated for a long time. When Josh and Lisa pulled apart, it was clear to see that the captain's wife was indeed with child. Captain Scott put his hand on his wife's stomach and smiled into her eyes. He thought of the prophecy made by Diviña in Dublin and declared, " We might want to consider a girl's name for this child. I have a strong feeling that this one's going to be a bonnie little lass." Tara felt as if she already knew Lisa. The woman was beautiful and, did indeed, look just like the figurehead on the prow of the ship.

After introductions were made, Captain Scott invited the four to come home with him, but they declined and declared that they would say their farewells at the dock.

"It would be no trouble, and I'd like Lisa to get to know you," he urged.

"You have been so kind to us, Josh, but we have a ways to go yet," said Tara. 'Tis best that we keep moving. 'Twould not be good to dally too long, if we are going to find my folks before the weather turns cold on us."

"According to the map you gave us, we have over a hundred and fifty miles of rugged overland trails and the waters of the Northumberland Strait to cross before we reach Tara's family in Prince Edward Island," added John.

"It's not a far distance that separates us," said Josh. "I have a feeling that we'll meet again one of these days. I want you to know that I count you, along with Jack and Rita, my good friends. The next time I'm in Dublin, John, I'll be sure to get word to your mother that all my passengers arrived safely, and that our trip across the Atlantic was most extraordinary."

It had already been decided that Tara would speak for the group to express their heartfelt thanks. "We'll write to you, Captain, and let you know that we're safe on the island with my family," promised Tara. "You extended not only your kindness, but shared everything that you had with us. You asked nothing in return for this gesture. You're a fine gentleman, sir, in the truest sense of the word. It is our dearest wish that your unselfish generosity toward us is rewarded, and that good fortune will follow you always."

Tara and Shauna proudly presented Captain Scott and his wife Lisa with an embroidered Irish blessing.

Buddy had donated a patch of canvas used to repair the sails, and Shauna contributed the use of her needles and some black, green, and gold thread from her sewing kit. Lovingly, the girls had stitched the prayer onto the canvas. A green shamrock completed the tapestry. John and Danny stretched the cloth onto a frame from wooden scraps used for ship repairs.

When all was said and done, the stitching looked quite lovely, and even as Josh accepted the gift from Tara, he knew it would become a family heirloom.

"We are honored to have this beautiful blessing grace our home," said Lisa.

"It will serve as a wonderful remembrance of a remarkable voyage," added Josh affectionately.

An Irish Blessing

May the road rise to meet you.
May the wind be always at your back.
May the sunshine warm your face.
The rain fall soft on your fields.
And until we meet again,
May God hold you
In the palm of His hand.

The friends unloaded the last of their humble belongings from the ship and packed them onto Maggie's back. Standing near Lisa and his three sons, Josh waved one last time as the four courageous friends, a small dog, and a horse walked slowly toward the town of St. John to buy a few supplies for the last leg of their journey.

Chapter 18 ~ August 1848 - New Brunswick

The friends pooled their money and found that they had a little over fourteen shillings between them. At a small general store in the center of town, they encountered an agreeable merchant known as Mr. Bruce. He took four shillings in payment for the provisions they would need for the long journey through the forested wilderness. The rest of their savings would be used to pay passage on a barge or ferry to cross the two bays that would take them to the island. They purchased four blankets, a pot and a frying pan, four tin plates and cups, a small metal box filled with matches, one ten-pound sack of dried cornmeal, a box of tea, salt, and a hunting knife. Mr. Bruce was a little uneasy that they could not afford a rifle. "This here land is untamed and many wild animals make the area their home. It'll be mighty important to stay together and keep a campfire burning all night. The wilderness is loaded with black bear, wildcats, moose, deer, and many small game animals. The fire will discourage unwanted critters from takin' yer food. You'd best sleep in shifts and throw wood on the fire throughout the night."

Mr. Bruce warned them to stay clear of a black and white critter with a bushy tail, known as a skunk. "Ya might git sprayed by that varmint, and the stink will cling to ya like a bottle of cheap French perfume. Washin' in a crick won't shake the smell off ya, no sir. That stench would surely gag a maggot," he said chuckling at his own humor.

After several days in the wilderness, a pattern took over the routine of each day. They broke camp at daybreak. Danny made sure that the fire was covered with wet dirt. An uncontrolled fire was the fear of anyone journeying through a forest. Mr. Bruce had told them that a few years earlier a large fire to the west had been fanned by a hurricane, and had destroyed a vast area of land before it died out. Tara and Shauna worked as a team to pack up their supplies. John loaded their provisions onto Maggie, and the four covered as much ground as they could before breaking for lunch around noon. They ate leftover Johnnycakes made from cornmeal and water from the previous night's dinner, and any berries they might happen to find along the way. After resting Maggie for an hour, they would travel until the shadows slanted, and the sun was slowly sinking in the west.

The time passed pleasantly. John amused the others with stories of his adventures living with the Tinkers. He could juggle anything while he walked. Sometimes he would play a lively tune on his whistle to pick up the spirits when someone got tired. Each was restless to learn more about the tales that chronicled their young lives. The stories made the walking less tedious.

When I was fifteen, Mam and I were camped in Dublin during a fair when a short barrel-shaped Russian named Alexi approached our camp with a large black bear. He dragged the unhappy creature toward us with a heavy iron chain attached to a collar around its huge neck. We watched, with some apprehension, as the unhappy bear growled in anguish.

We had seen this man and his bear perform at the fair earlier in the week as part of a traveling circus troupe, but this animal did not resemble the clever creature we had enjoyed as members of the audience. The act had been quite clever. The bear could balance a ball on its nose and push a monkey in a cart at the commands of its Russian master who gave it treats of small fish. Mam and I jumped to our feet as the man frantically shouted in his native language. The confused looks on our faces must have alerted his reason for coming because he began speaking in broken English.

"Excuse ignorance for speaking in native language. My name Alexi. You must help Sonia," the Russian begged. "Sonia very sick. People say that Tinker woman good with healing."

Mam looked at the man and said, "We will be happy to help your friend Sonia, but where is she?"

"Sonia is here!" yelled the Russian in frantic tones, and he pointed to the wretched creature, just as the bear tried to knock over a log near our fire. "It will be better soon, darling Sonia. Daddy will get help for your pain."

Mam and I took a step backward when it became clear to us that Alexi wanted Mam to perform some medical treatment on his trained bear, Sonia.

"Are you daft, man? My mother uses her skills to treat people. What can she possibly do for your, Sonia?" I inquired pointing to a bear which was in obvious pain.

"I do not know, but I am sick with worry. You must help me," Alexi pleaded.

Mam had been fairly quiet. I could see her study the bear as it picked up a branch and began chewing and grimacing all at the same time. At length she spoke.

"I think I know what is wrong with Sonia," she smiled. "It looks to me as if Sonia might have a toothache. Look at the way she's clawing at her right jaw. It looks to be swollen on that side as well."

"This may be true," the Russian brightened. "I must confess, my darling Sonia have passion for tea with lots of sugar. I know I should not give, but she love so much," he added looking with longing at his beloved bear.

"I have some experience pulling septic teeth," informed Mam, "but I do not know how I could be of service to you. How would I be able to get her mouth open so that I might perform the procedure?"

The Russian looked to the ground with shoulders that sagged. Soon his head shot up and he was smiling.

"I have answer for problem. Sonia also have passion for something that will help her sleep so you might have look into mouth. You see…my Sonia has great fondness for vodka!"

"What is that?" I asked.

"Vodka is national drink of Russia. It strong liquor made from your beloved potatoes. We Russians have fondness for potatoes like Irish. Sometime we eat potato; sometimes we make into clear liquid that we drink called vodka. Problem for me…I have no vodka left from supplies brought from homeland, and I have not found this drink in your beautiful Ireland."

Mam and I could hardly contain our laughter, but we knew that to laugh would cause the Russian some embarrassment, so Mam asked in gentle tones. "Do you think that your Sonia might like our national drink? It's called Irish whiskey."

"I have tried this Irish whiskey, and believe it to be almost as fine a drink as vodka. Never have I given this whiskey to Sonia, but we must try. Sonia must get better, or we will not be able to earn our keep with other members of our group. I go buy large bottle of this Irish drink called whiskey."

The Russian tied Sonia to a nearby tree and ran off to purchase the whiskey. He soon returned with a bottle of the amber liquid. He offered a small cup to Sonia, but she was clearly not impressed with the liquor and refused the drink by slapping the cup to the ground. The Russian was so sad I thought that he might cry, but fortunately Mam came up with the perfect solution.

"Alexi, you mentioned that Sonia has a great liking for tea with sugar," Mam remarked. "What if we brew a large kettle of tea and lace it with sugar and the whiskey. Sonia might take to the whiskey if it is disguised in the sweet tea."

"Idea good. We try," said the Russian.

Sonia lapped up the brew like it was milk and honey. She had consumed nearly a gallon of the nectar, and was soon staggering around our camp like a drunken sailor on a ship. Alexi spoke to her in soothing Russian tones until she dropped to the ground, rolled onto her back, and began to snore. Mam and I quickly sprang to action. We did not want to have the effects of the liquor wear off before we could pull the infected tooth out of Sonia's mouth.

"How were you able to pry the jaws of the beast open?" asked Danny in horror. "Weren't you afraid you might lose a hand?"

"Ah, now that was the cleverness of it." John looked at the others and winked.

"Alexi helped us open Sonia's mouth, I nearly choked as a bellow of hot septic breath poured from the snoring cavity of the drunken bear. The alert Russian quickly wedged a stout log into the uninfected side of her jaw. With haste, Mam found the bothersome incisor and attached a clamp to the base of the tooth. I knew that Mam would not have the strength to pull out the offensive root. So Alexi and I began the task of prying it out of Sonia's mouth. I braced myself by planting my legs astride the huge neck of creature and pulled until the veins popped out in my neck and sweat poured from by brow. I felt certain that the beast would surely rise up and slap me to the ground with her paw, but she lay motionless in her unconscious stupor. Taking turns at the chore, it took Alexi and I the better part of thirty minutes to yank the rotten fang from the bear's jaw. The whiskey had done its deed, and Sonia never twitched a muscle as the bloody tooth released from its place in her mouth. The bear moaned once but continued to sleep for the next hour. The last sight I remember was Alexi and four of his countrymen carrying Sonia away from our camp on a makeshift stretcher."

John sighed. "The next time I saw Alexi, he was proudly wearing the polished bear tooth around his neck, which had been wired to a leather cord. A happier Sonia could once more perform for her supper. Mam suggested that Alexi might want to stop giving the bear sugar in her tea, but I don't know if he ever took her advice, for a few days later the fair ended and we moved on. I never saw Alexi or Sonia again."

"I think it's sad that the bear was made to perform tricks for her master. I believe Sonia would have been happier if she had been allowed to roam free," said Tara sadly.

"I agree with you Tara," said John. "An enslaved wild beast performing tricks for little bites of fish seems out of harmony with nature."

Traveling through the forests of New Brunswick, the four travelers witnessed scores of animals. Rabbit, beavers, squirrels, and martins made the area their home. They walked along a roughly cleared trail, which was used to carry mail from St. John to a few logging towns to the north. The four had covered a fair distance and decided to camp just off the trail by a gentle creek that ran through a meadow near a wooded area.

"The last part of our journey will prove to be the hardest," said John, as the four sat around a fire cooking their evening meal. John's experience, living with the Tinkers, had been invaluable to the group. He knew how to live off the land. Diviña had packed his slingshot, and earlier in the day he had brought down a pheasant and a partridge for their supper.

"I can't believe that I'm eating the very bird that the squire raised so carefully on his estate," said Danny. I haven't enjoyed the taste of pheasant since my Da poached the occasional bird when I was just a wee lad. I thought about poaching one from Dellamort Wood, but I was too afraid that I might lose my job."

"Imagine the shooting party that the squire could give for all his muckity-muck friends in this grand forest," added Shauna. "There are so many game birds here, and they seem ready for the taking!"

"'Tis absolutely true. These woods are filled with enough food to feed all the hungry people of Ireland," remarked Tara.

Tara had found the mosquitoes quite bothersome, especially when the sun began to set. Luckily the smoke from their campfire seemed to keep them at bay. It was a bonus to have Maggie carry most of their supplies, and Tara was just as happy to walk. She carried the bottle, strapped in its leather pouch, across her shoulder and under her arm. It gave her an extraordinary measure of comfort to have it to her side.

The Emerald Bottle had long since completed its metamorphose. Its color was primarily emerald green, while hues of lime, gold, moss, and jade added to its complexity. A few faint streaks of blue were all that remained of the sapphire color it had once been in John and Diviña's caravan. All four friends had studied the bottle in great detail. It was impossible to discern what substance formed the intricate pattern of the layers. The pigment of its surface was as hard and lustrous as a precious jewel and equally as beautiful. It appeared that the interior of the bottle was glass, but it seemed strong and able to withstand rough handling. Tara was in awe of its beauty. Every day she promised herself to remain worthy of being entrusted with the mystery of its energy.

John sat near the fire carefully whittling another groove into a long spear he had made with the hunting knife. The notches would mark the days on the trail until they reached their destination. Danny roasted the pheasant and partridge on a spit centered between two fork-like sticks. Earlier, Tara had picked some wild sage she found near the trail, and she had helped Shauna stuff it into the cavity of the birds. The savory smell filled the air as the skin turned a crisp golden brown. The pungent odor made everyone hungry. Earlier they had discovered a patch of wild blueberries. They picked some to eat, and filled the cooking pot, which had been a gift from Little Joe, with the rest for a treat after their meal. Shauna boiled a large pan of water for tea while Bailey hung close to Danny as he cooked the meat.

Bailey had learned the hard way to stay close at hand. On their first day out, he was chasing a rabbit and came face to face with a porcupine. He yelped as four quills stuck into the top of his head. His whining continued as John dug them out. Tara made a poultice of pulverized birch bark to help with the pain and swelling.

Josh and Buddy had mapped out a trail for the travelers. They would follow a rough road along the western shore of the Bay of Fundy that was used to bring supplies and mail to some northern logging towns. From there they would catch a logging barge across the bay into Nova Scotia. Buddy told them that from a place called Maccan there was a good stagecoach road that would lead them to the small seaside town of Pictou. From there, they might not have to wait too long to hook passage on a logging vessel that would take them to Murray Harbor, located on the southeast end of Prince Edward Island.

"If we can travel ten miles a day, we might make it to your folks' place in two to three weeks," offered John. Tara had been given a hand-drawn map in one of the letters written by her folks. It described how to get to Uncle Pat's farm, located on the Vernon River near Fort Augustus.

Tara could not believe that soon she would be able to hold and hug her family after the many months of loneliness and separation. A bubble of happiness swelled inside her chest, which erupted into song most of the day.

"I never knew you had such a lovely voice," praised Shauna. "I don't think I ever heard you sing when you worked on the estate."

"I didn't," expressed Tara to her friend. "I suppose I was just too lonely and scared."

"John," asked Tara as she stood near the fire watching Danny roast the birds, "how long do you think 'tis until we finally reach the logging town that Josh and Buddy told you about?"

"We've been on the trail making good progress for three days, Tara. If we continue at this pace, I think we could be there in two to three more days. Then we will have to wait and see what means of transportation we can secure to take us into Nova Scotia."

"This meat looks to be just about perfect," announced Danny, which is good because Bailey is about to drool the flames clear out."

At that moment the four campers heard the crackling of brush and leaves coming from the direction of the woods. The hairs on the back of John's neck raised, and he stood and grabbed the spear he had been carving notches on into his hands. Danny quickly picked up his spear and turned toward the direction of the sound. A low growl erupted from Bailey as each girl reached for her walking stick. Tara thought that a bear might be attracted to the camp by the smell of the meat. Instinctively she moved closer to the fire, and Shauna followed her lead.

Several branches moved, and an Indian stepped into the clearing. He wore buckskin leggings, a breechcloth apron, a deerskin shirt, and moccasins. His black hair was worn loose over his shoulders. A leather cord tied around his forehead held it in place. His skin was the color of stained cherry wood. High cheekbones framed a straight nose and dark brown eyes that were opened wide with apprehension. The young native's uneasiness in the presence of the campers was reflected in his handsome face. Slowly the Indian placed his bow and arrow, a long reed that looked like a hollowed out pipe, and a leather bag on the ground. He stood up and stepped away from the weapons. Waiting for someone to speak, the Indian seemed nervous and proud at the same time.

The group remained frozen for several seconds until it occurred to Tara that something was amiss, and the man that stood before them was not a threat to their safety. She was the first to speak. "Good evening to you, sir, please come and sit with us by our fire. Are you hungry?" Tara gestured toward the campfire. She made eating motions with her hands in an effort to appear friendly.

The man looked directly at Tara and spoke. "My name Anaki. I come long distance from there." He pointed to the south. Anaki looked over his shoulder and waved for someone to join him. A woman holding a baby stepped into the clearing. Although she tried to smile, it was clear that she was very distressed. She made her way to Anaki and stood next to him. She wore a deerskin dress and soft leather boots. Her black hair was parted in the middle and tied with leather straps on each side of her ears. The baby, who looked to be about a year old, was wrapped in a gray woolen blanket and appeared to be sleeping. "This is wife. Her name, Takis. Our son, Manankas." Takis smiled nervously at Tara as she handed over the baby with an imploring look.

Tara looked at the baby, and felt his forehead. "This infant is burning with fever." There was a rattling in the chest area, and he was having difficulty breathing. Tara looked at Anaki and asked, "Your baby is very sick. How long has he been like this?"

"Three days." Anaki held up three fingers, "Manankas stop eat, stop drink. Hot in head. Baby too sick, not cry for two days, only sleep, breathe hard."

Shauna came forward and invited the couple to join them around the campfire. Anaki guided his wife into the area warmed by the fire, and helped her to sit down. Takis never took her eyes off of Tara, as the Irish girl placed the baby on one of their blankets and carefully removed the gray blanket from the feverish infant. The baby was limp and unresponsive.

"I have no skill with babies, but I do have some knowledge of healing herbs. I will do what I can for your child," promised Tara. John brought Tara her bag of herbs, and Tara asked Shauna to bring over some of the hot water from the pot they had been boiling for tea. Quickly she made a brew of birch bark tea mixed with dried lavender. She cradled the baby in her arms and placed drops of the liquid into his mouth. Tara looked at Anaki and Takis, and asked, "What brought you to our camp?"

Anaki spoke to his wife in his native language. She spoke quickly to him and nodded. Together they turned to the others. "Wife not sleep much since baby take sick. Last night wife very tired. Fall to sleep with baby in arms. Takis have strange dream. Have vision of young girl with hair color of raven, and eyes like pool of deep water. Girl smile, hold green pot that sparkle like shiny stone. Blue Eyes wave for Takis to come to her for help."

Anaki continued his spellbinding tale. "We walk all day. Worry much that son will die. We hungry, but too sad to eat. Then, we follow smell of meat cooking in distance. It bring us to this place. Takis see your face near fire from forest. Wife say you look like girl in dream."

Tara looked at John and the others for a few seconds. It seemed as though the forest had stopped breathing. Slowly she placed Manankas on the blanket, and with everyone watching her, she reverently removed the bottle from its case. A gasp and then a relieved sigh issued from Takis's lungs. She spoke excitedly to Anaki in their language. Tara gathered the baby and the blanket close to her. She picked up the bottle and placed it near the baby's chest. Then, she wrapped the baby and bottle in the blanket and hugged them both to her. Somehow she knew that this is what she needed to do. It seemed that the baby began to breathe a little easier. All they could do was wait, and hope that the bottle would help the sick child.

The couple was invited to join the friends for dinner. Anaki said they had not eaten much since the baby had taken sick. He told them that they had lived in the area of their ancestral tribe, known as Mohegan, in a place called Connecticut, and that he had learned to speak some English at a missionary school when he was a small boy.

"One day, man come to our village and say that Great American White Father pass law. Say all our people must be taken in path of setting sun to place called Wisconsin. Many people cry. Old, young, brave warriors, and women taken west to new land. Some people hide. Many years we hide with our people in forest. Life for Mohegan very hard. Some get found, taken to Wisconsin place. After last winter snow, we come north with son to find others of our people who have made same journey guided by North Star.

Tara shook her head slowly as she listened. Tara thought their story seemed so very much like the story of her own people, driven from their land and forced to find a new home. Somehow she sensed that life for the Indians was only going to get harder. As she held Manankas, she continued to place tiny drops of the herbal water on his tongue. She noticed that his breathing didn't seem as raspy, and he began to lap at the liquid with his tongue. After Takis had eaten some of the food, she came over to Tara and motioned that she would take the baby so that Tara could eat. Tara handed her the bundle and the birch bark water. Takis smiled and spoke to her husband.

"Takis say that Manankas is much resting than before. Wife think Great Spirit guide us to this place."

The group talked long into the night. By the time they decided to get some sleep, Manankas was clearly better. He was not as feverish and his breathing was almost normal.

In the morning, the baby seemed nearly well. Takis nursed the baby, and he took her milk for the first time in days. The couple was invited to stay with the group until the friends had to make their way east to the coast to cross the bay. Takis and Anaki said they would be pleased to travel north with them. "Place we go to, very cold. We must move swift like deer, or not make before snow come. Go to land where white man not want to live. Hunt in peace. Live in old ways of ancestors."

As the travelers made their way up the trail, the young natives shared a variety of useful information with their new friends. Anaki showed them how the long hollowed pipe was used. The reed had been dried and decorated with strips of deer hide. He demonstrated how to use the blowgun to bring down two rabbits that were running in a shrub area. He was very adept with the weapon. He was just as skillful with his bow and arrow, and the group had plenty to eat for their meals. John displayed his skill with the slingshot, and Anaki nodded in a gesture of approval. Takis showed the various uses of some of the plants that Tara and Shauna were not familiar with. She demonstrated, using sign language or with Anaki's help, the ones to stay clear from, and the ones that were good to eat or to use as healing medicine.

After two days, they camped at the place where they would part ways in the morning. All day the girls had gathered blueberries and wild strawberries for a special farewell feast. Anaki had killed a wild turkey with his bow and arrow, and John contributed two rabbits to the dinner. They found a suitable camp area near a small swift stream. By now, Manankas was completely well. Bailey had taken a special interest in the small boy, and they played together on a blanket while the others prepared the evening meal.

"Tall friend, play wooden pipe for celebration," requested Anaki. He was very fond of the sound of the flute. John picked up his whistle and began to play a lovely tune while Danny roasted the meat and the girls watched Manankas and Bailey.

At length, Takis said something to Anaki. He nodded, and together they walked over to get something out of her satchel. Anaki and Takis strolled over to Tara and presented her with the most beautiful rectangular shaped wooden basket that Tara had ever seen. The basket was about nine inches long and six inches wide. Its height was about the same size as its width. Some of bark on the front of the basket had been carefully scraped away to reveal a lighter colored pattern in a scroll-like design.

"Takis," said Tara, "this basket is lovely."

"Takis make box from bark of birch tree. It custom of our people. Takis want Tara to take as gift for giving *orenda*, life force, back to Manankas," said Anaki proudly. "It give great honor to her for you to take."

Tara was overcome with emotion. This couple, who had suffered so much and had so little, wanted to give her something as precious to them as Granny Cassie's Belleek had been to her. Somehow, Tara knew that it would dishonor Takis if she did not graciously accept her gift. She turned to the young woman and said, "Thank you, Takis. I will treasure the box all my life. A part of you and your family will be with me always." Anaki translated Tara's sentiments as Tara leaned over and kissed the young Indian girl on the cheek. Takis radiated a warm smile through tear-filled eyes. "I only wish I had something to give to you," said Tara sadly, "but I have nothing…"

At that moment John stepped forward and said, "I do. Anaki, please take this whistle to remember the time that we have spent together. Please know that we are your friends."

Anaki smiled and said, "You give Anaki and family great honor. I try to learn to play like tall friend. Pray to Great Spirit for guidance. Pray that Takis and Manankas have patience with Anaki, like crane that wait for fish to swim near for supper."

He laughed. Tara looked at John with gratitude. She knew how much he loved his whistle.

Later after dinner, Tara had a chance to spend a few moments alone with John as she washed the pans in the stream, and he was returning from the forest with more wood for the fire. "Thank you, John for helping me, once again. I know what your whistle means to you. You must be weary of coming to my aid over and over."

"Let's just say that I knew how much you wanted to return their warm gesture of kinship. I can get another whistle one day. I learned many things from Diviña, but the lesson I learned most of all is that *things* are not important. Material things can always be replaced. People are important Tara," said John earnestly.

Tara was reminded of the aura of wisdom that seemed to surround Diviña, and she was not surprised that John had been impressed by her words. "Anyway, I knew how much Anaki admired it these past days. He couldn't take his eyes off the thing. It gave me pleasure to do it, lass. I must say, I'm glad he didn't take a fancy to my fiddle. I don't know if I could have been as generous," he laughed.

The travelers spent a day resting at a small logging camp called Point Albert. They treated themselves to a night's lodging at an inn, which was really nothing more than a log cabin, and a hot meal of fried codfish and potatoes. The next day, everyone was in good spirits when they paid two shillings for passage on a logging barge across the bay that would take four passengers and one horse into Nova Scotia. The captain said that Bailey was so small he could ride for free. The six mile trip took about an hour. From there they followed a fairly decent road used by a stagecoach company to transport passengers and mail across the Cumberland into the harbor town of Pictou. According to the markings on John's spear, they had been on the road for two weeks. A stagecoach driver at one of the stops said they could ride to Pictou on his coach for two shillings, but the friends decided it would be better to save their money and use their legs for transportation. They had second thoughts about the offer when it started to rain.

The group had experienced a few summer showers over the past weeks, but nothing like this deluge. It was miserable. The rain poured in sheets and drenched their clothes and hair. The only good thing about the rain was that it kept the bothersome mosquitoes away. All they could do was make the best of the situation and keep moving. On the sixteenth day, the group came to a creek that had swollen into a swift-flowing river. John looked up at the sky, "It doesn't look like this rain is going to stop anytime soon. Let me find a place shallow enough to cross downstream."

He returned after twenty minutes, and reported to his weary companions. "There's a fairly good crossing that's only thirty yards wide, about a quarter of a mile downstream. The water runs fast, but it looks fairly shallow. If we stick together, I think we can make it across without any problems."

John gave instructions to the others. "I'll test the crossing by walking Maggie to the other side. I'll carry Bailey in the knapsack Mam made for him. When I'm safely across the bank, I'll wave. That'll be the signal for you to start. I'll meet you in the middle of the river to help." Everyone nodded in agreement.

John waded into the water. The stream ran swiftly but, at its deepest, it only came up to his waist. He got to shore and waved the others across while he waded out to meet them in the middle. Shauna went first, then Tara, followed by Danny. The icy cold water was very swift, and Tara's skirt became heavy and cumbersome. She was a strong swimmer and not overly worried. She sensed that the current was gradually dragging them downstream. Tara looked back to check on Danny. It was clear to Tara that Danny was uncomfortable as the water rose above his waist and crept up to his shoulders. Suddenly, she remembered that Danny could not swim. She had the foreboding feeling that he might be swept downstream into deeper water if she did not act quickly. John had the same thought because he started rushing toward Shauna to grab her hand.

"Shauna!" he shouted. "Grab hands and form a human chain. You're being pulled into deeper water."

Shauna nodded and reached for Tara's hand. Tara turned to complete the link with Danny. "Take my hand Danny!" she shouted over the roar of the water.

Danny looked wide-eyed with panic as he reached to take Tara's outstretched hand. Just as he touched the tip of her fingers he disappeared under water. Tara looked at Shauna who was beginning to show signs of strain on her own face.

Luckily, John found her and pulled her toward him.

Go to the bank!" Tara implored as she turned and let the current carry her in the direction of her distressed friend.

Danny came up sputtering just out of Tara's reach. She knew she had to throw him a lifeline. All she had was the Emerald Bottle secured to the strap on her shoulder. The water was cold and her hands numb as she struggled to lift it over her head. The look on Danny's face made her sick with fear. Tara held the strap and tossed the bottle in his direction. He lunged at her first attempt but the bottle slipped out of his grasp, and he sank under the water for a few seconds. Tara kicked her legs faster in a skirt that hindered her progress. She tossed the bottle a second time, and he was able to clutch it between his hands.

Tara was tethered to him at last, and was determined that she would stay that way. "Danny, you *must* listen to me. 'Tis your very life that depends on it. This bottle is hollow," she whispered in a confident voice. "It'll keep us afloat. but you must relax your body and let the bottle do its work. Do you understand?"

Danny nodded his head, but could not force his body to follow her instruction. Tara spoke to him in soothing tones. "Listen to me, Danny. Can you feel the buoyancy of the bottle?" Danny nodded. "Good. Look at me Danny. Look right into my eyes."

Tara spoke until she could feel Danny's body begin to relax. She knew it was vital to keep talking. "I feel certain that we'll come to a place on this river where 'twill not be so deep. I am thinkin' that we should let the bottle take us to that very spot. From there, we can wade to the other side of the bank and meet John and Shauna." Danny nodded again but did not speak. Tara continued to talk about Shauna, and what a grand girl she was. The sheer look of panic began to fade from her friend's face and they floated for a while longer. Suddenly, they came to a shallow place in the river, as Tara had predicted, where they could stand. Together, they made their way to the east side of the swollen stream and collapsed onto the mossy bank. Neither of them could stand. Their legs were like limp rags. "We'll just rest here a wee bit before we make our way back up stream."

It took Tara and Danny about fifteen minutes before they had enough strength to follow the stream north and find John and Shauna. They walked for some time before hearing the shouts of their friends calling their names. "We're here!" signaled Tara in a voice weakened by cold and exhaustion.

When the four finally met up, they hugged and fell onto the wet grass. Bailey jumped on Tara and licked her face. "I know, boy," she told him, "'tis glad I am to see you too."

"Shauna and I discovered a cave not too far from here," said John. "Let's go and get out of this rain." John had Danny lean on him for support, as Shauna guided Tara to a cave that might once have been home to a hibernating bear. It was large enough for all of them, including Maggie, to find shelter from the rain. "I hope these matches are still dry," said John as he opened the tin box and started a fire. Luckily, there was enough dry grass and kindling inside the cave to get a small fire going. They fed the flames with small sticks and branches until finally it grew into a sizable blaze. The heat from the fire slowly began to warm their bodies, and they huddled close to its core in their blankets. Tara sensed that Danny had gone into shock, because he had fallen asleep almost immediately. She checked on him from time to time, but his color was good, and he was not shivering.

"'Twas a fine brave thing you did Tara," praised Shauna. "I think Danny would be singin' with the angels now if not for you."

"How ever did you manage to keep him afloat?" asked John.

"'Twas the strangest thing. I knew I had to fasten myself to him, so I threw the bottle to him and held on to the strap. That wee bottle kept us afloat, but for the life of me I don't know how. The bottle was empty. I was plannin' to fill it once we reached the other side of the river. Still, it doesn't quite make sense to me. My skirt was so heavy. It didn't seem possible that the wee vessel could support the weight of us both, but it held us up like a fisherman's buoy until we came to the shallow place where we were able to stagger to the shore."

Shauna made some tea and corn cakes, and the tired friends rested in the warmth of the cave until daybreak. Danny slept for ten hours, but when he awoke in the morning his mood matched the sparkling sun glistening on the leaves of the trees. "I thought I was going to drown, to be sure, Tara. Had it not been for your bottle keepin' me afloat, I would've gone under. When we get to the island, I'm going to have you teach me to swim." The three agreed that they would help Danny learn.

The group found their way back to the main road and made good time traveling for two more days without further trouble. "Look yonder!" shouted Danny with joy. "We're here." The four stood on a hill and recognized the narrow stretch of sea in the distance. "It's the Northumberland Strait just as Buddy marked it on his map." Thirty minutes later they entered the seaside town of Pictou tired and happy. The notches on John's spear showed that the friend's had been traveling through the wilderness for twenty days.

Chapter 19 ~ August 1848 - Murray Harbor

Pictou was a thriving little harbor town used for transporting lumber to Europe. A booming fishing industry also brought income to many of the people who had settled the area. The travelers got lucky and found the captain of a lumber vessel who was sailing to Murray Harbor with the afternoon tide. The captain said he would take on passengers for the twenty-mile trip across the Northumberland Strait for four shillings.

John had to do some fancy bargaining to convince Captain McRae that four shillings was a might steep, as it was all the money they had left. During the bartering, good fortune smiled on the travelers again. John, offhandedly, mentioned the name of Captain Joshua Scott. McRae knew Josh and respected him greatly. He astonished the four by agreeing to take them across the water for half the usual fair and John gratefully pressed two shillings into his hand.

"Any friend of Captain Scott is a friend of mine." Captain McRae invited the four on board his ship for a bite to eat. The young friends told the captain about their remarkable trip across the Atlantic. "That was an amazing bit o' good luck. Josh is a fine man and a worthy seaman. Twenty-seven days sailing west is a *very* fast trip for cert. I've heard tales about the strange light known as St. Elmo's Fire, but 'tis a very rare sight to encounter. I will enjoy sharing these stories with my mates. We love to swap sea tales. When I run into Captain Scott, I'll relay that I sailed you safely to the island." The friends thanked the captain for his kindness.

The voyage across the strait was filled with excitement for Tara. She could scarcely concentrate as Captain McRae told the young friends about the many Irish who had settled the land. "Unlike New Brunswick and Nova Scotia, the island does not have the dense forested land, so the land is perfectly suited for farming. The fertile red soil is grand for growing potatoes and many other crops. There are low rolling hills that will remind you of your beloved motherland. Land is cheap. Any man willing to work the soil can make a decent life and own the land that he toils."

Tara held Bailey in her arms. When the island came into view, Tara could see low cliffs rise up along the shore with gentle rolling hills in the background. All four friends were struck speechless with the similarity to their own dear Ireland. Various shades of greens mixed with the reddish-brown earth made a bittersweet scene in the distance, as Tara thought of the struggles in Ireland. Silent tears streamed down Tara's cheeks. She was overcome with emotion. *I'm here, and soon I'll get to hold my family in my arms.* Shauna moved closer to stand next to her friend. The boys soon followed until they all stood together. Without words being spoken, the four friends linked arms and stood together in silent wonder. Their long journey would soon be over.

Murray Harbor was a small port located on the southeast side of the island. A friendly fisherman pointed them in the direction of Uncle Pat's farm on the Vernon River. "Head north on that road until you come to Fort Augustus. Your uncle's farm is just west of the fort on the Vernon River. Folks are neighborly around here, so you should have no trouble finding your family." Tara thanked the fisherman and told him her father had sent her a map with landmarks which would help them.

A farmer who had just unloaded a wagon of produce in Murray Harbor stopped to talk to the young travelers. "'Tis new to the island are ya, friends?" he asked. "Where're ya headed?"

"We are on our way to my relative's farm up along the Vernon River," said Tara. "Maybe you know them. Patrick and Katie Connolly?"

"Of course I know them. Wait a minute, you're not the daughter of Michael and Elsie Maguire?"

"Why, yes I am," said Tara smiling, "My name is Tara Maguire."

"Saints preserve us. We have been hoping to get word that you were on your way. Your folks have been a wee bit worried about you, Tara. 'Tis a grand looking lass you are with the lovely dark hair and blue eyes. But wait, where are my manners? My name is Sean Vaughn from County Clare, Ireland. I used to own a small pub in Lahinch, but moved to the island in 1832. Hop onto my wagon, and I'll give ya a wee lift up the road to my farm. You can stay with my wife, Bridget, and me tonight, and we'll drive ya over to Katie and Pat's place in the mornin'."

Introductions were made. John tied Maggie to the back of the wagon. John and Danny rode in the back of the wagon, while Shauna, Tara, and Bailey squeezed onto the buckboard with Sean. He filled Tara in on the latest news of her family. "Your Pa just put a down payment on a dear parcel of land over in Tracadie. He'll begin building his home after the potato harvest is completed. In fact, the folks in this area are going to help him with a barn raising in a few weeks." He looked back at John and Danny. "You strong lads will come in mighty handy. Are ya plannin' to settle here?"

Danny and John looked at each other before John spoke. "We hadn't really talked too much about our plans for the future. I know nothing of farming, but Danny here knows a fair bit about livestock, and horses in particular. I guess we'll just have to wait and see what develops. 'Tis a dream I've had of owning my own land, though. I've never stayed in one place too long," he added. "I've been on the move most of my life. I like the notion of setting down roots somewhere."

"The rich red soil on the island is our greatest resource. We rotate our crops with potatoes, oats, barley, and other grains so that the soil stays healthy and strong. Fishin' is a grand way to make your livelihood, if you're so inclined. There are plenty of lobster, clams, and cod in the waters offshore. And the game, lads! If you have any skill with the rifle, there are partridges, ring-neck pheasants, snipes, and rabbits for the pluckin'. No man could ever go hungry on this island. Ah, but the land, lads," he beamed, "I own one hundred and thirty acres of prime farm land, and a small wooded area with a creek runnin' through. Never in my wildest dreams did I think that I would be the master of my own estate!" he boasted proudly. "When I think of all the poor folk in Ireland struggling to work as tenant farmers...." Sean broke his thought as if reflecting on some distant memories.

"My Da was a tenant farmer, and died working on someone else's estate," offered Shauna in quiet tones.

"I'm sorry for your troubles, lass," Mr. Vaughn said with sincerity, "I hope you carve out a better life for yourself here."

Sean and Bridget Vaughn had a comfortable home near a place called Brown's Creek. All of their children were grown and married, with farms of their own in the same area. Bridget, who reminded Shauna and Tara of Mrs. Larkin, loaned the girls some clothes so that she could wash and repair the ones they were wearing. "Ya can't be greetin' your folks without looking your best," she lectured. She filled a large bathtub with steaming water, and the girls were treated to the luxury of a hot bath. The boys preferred to bathe in the creek to give the lasses some privacy. Bridget insisted that she would wash the boys' clothes as well.

By the time supper was served, the four young friends, seated around the dining room table, were scrubbed and polished to a shine. "I must say, you're a handsome group. It makes me miss my own darlin' children who are grown and living on their own farms now," sighed Bridget.

There was no lack of conversation at dinner. The four friends shared the adventure of leaving Squire Dellamort's estate, the voyage on Captain Scott's ship, and their trek through the wildernesses of New Brunswick and Nova Scotia.

By the time Tara crawled into bed with Shauna, she was exhausted. Shauna was asleep almost instantly, but Tara, who was too excited, decided to pray to her patron saint.

Dearest St. Catherine, thank you for watching over us and guiding us to this beautiful island. Protect dear Father Scanlon and all the others who struggle with the troubles in Ireland. Thank you, Granny Cassie, for helping me find my path away from the squire's estate, and into the arms of all the dear friends who helped me come to this glorious isle to be reunited with my precious family. Amen. The words of the prayer calmed Tara, and she fell asleep with the whisper of the word, Amen.

The next morning was clear and sunny and mirrored Tara's mood. They headed to the kitchen and ate a hearty breakfast.

While the boys went with Sean to hitch the horse, the girls helped Bridget organized a picnic lunch. They loaded the basket onto the buckboard with Bridget, and Sean situated the four travelers and their belongings in the back of his wagon for the fifteen-mile trip to the Connolly farm. A tethered Maggie trotted behind. Everyone was in high spirits as Sean and Bridget pointed out various landmarks and farms along the way.

"I cannot believe how much this land reminds me of Ireland," said John.

"I know," responded Sean, "everyone who comes here says the same thing. 'Tis why so many Irish are attracted to the spot. We feel a kinship to the land and the other Irish who have settled here."

At Tara's request, John broke out his fiddle and played for the enjoyment of the group. Everyone harmonized to the lilting tunes that every Irish person knows by heart, and never tires of singing. Sean and Bridget stopped around midday for a picnic lunch in a grove of birch trees. Bridget was a wonderful cook. She laid out cold chicken, pickled cucumbers, mushroom hand pies, lemonade, and blueberry tarts.

John came over to sit near Tara as they ate. "You must be excited, Tara. You'll be with your family in a few hours. I'm very happy for you, lass."

"I'm almost too excited to eat, John, but 'tis glad that we have an opportunity to talk for a few minutes. I know how hectic things will get once we've reached Uncle Pat's farm. There are a few things I need to say to you, so please hear me out." John looked into Tara's eyes and thought she seemed so wise for her age. "I can never begin to thank you, John, for everything you've done for me. When I made the decision to leave Squire Dellamort's estate, I didn't know how I was going to make my way home to my family. In truth, I'd be dead if you hadn't found me in the woods. You saved my life. Then, you took me to Dublin, and stood up for me against the butler and the squire. You brought me across the Atlantic. You spent every penny you had, not to mention...giving away your lovely whistle," she quipped, "to get me and the others through the wilderness and across two bays to this lovely island. I know, with all my heart, that I could never have made this journey without you, John. Please know that I'm forever in your debt. I'll pray each night that the sacrifice you've made on *my* behalf will be rewarded in a way that makes you truly happy. And if you come to realize that your life is not of this island but back in Ireland, I will do everything to help you get home to your family. Whatever happens, I want you to know that I count you as my friend...my very good friend."

John looked at Tara and declared, "I'm not so sure that I'm deserving of such high praise. You're a remarkable young lass. I'm almost certain you'd have found a way to get home to your family. But you're right about a lot of it. 'Tis hard to believe that I've known you such a short time. The experiences we've shared, and the adventures we've been through, make me feel as though I've known you forever. Diviña believes nothing happens in the world by accident. She thought it was my destiny to make this journey, and I learned long ago to trust her instincts. We shall have to wait to see what the future holds. But please know, Tara, that I was happy to help you find your way to your family. It made me feel as though I was doing something worthy. Diviña...and even Shady Mary, helped me find my path in life. I would be dead now, had it not been for them. In helping you, I felt I was honoring them. Diviña taught me that everything we do in life is intertwined. Whatever happens, I know we'll always be friends." John looked over at the others then turned back to Tara. "Now eat, lass," he whispered, with a twinkle in his eye, "or Mrs. Vaughn will be thinkin' you don't like her cookin'!"

Chapter 20 ~ August 1848 - Connolly Farm

She saw him working in the fields. Working the land, like she had seen him do so many times on his own small farm in Ireland. He looked content…but then, he was always happiest when there was dirt on his hands and mud on his boots. He looked in the direction of the sound of the wagon. The sun was in his eyes, and he squinted to see who might be paying a visit to Pat and Katie on this fine August day. The wagon stopped, but still he could not imagine who it was. He leaned against his shovel, happy to take a break for a few minutes. A young woman got out of the back of the wagon and walked toward him while the others remained behind. His first thought was that the people were lost, and needed directions to find their way. But somewhere in the depth of his memory, the gait of her movements made him catch his breath. When she started to run, he dropped his shovel, and blindly moved to intercept her. She ran across the newly plowed field mindless of the dust collecting on the hem of her skirt. Tears streamed down her cheeks, but she was smiling as he gathered her into his arms.

"Tara, is it you? Is it really you…or saints preserve us, am I dreamin'?" he cried. "I have prayed for this moment every night for the past fourteen months. I can't believe that you're finally here in my arms."

"'Tis true, Da," she cried with joyful tears. "I'm truly home, and nothin' will ever separate us again."

Elsie took the washing off the line as Diane played near the wash basket with the handmade doll Katie had made for her third birthday. The twins were helping Uncle Pat grease a wagon wheel in the barn while Katie peeled potatoes in her kitchen for supper.

Pat and Katie had been unable to have any children of their own, and they loved their niece and nephews as though they were their own. A wagon pulled into the drive and stopped. Elsie was surprised to see Sean and Bridget Vaughn waving happily from their seats. "This is a lovely surprise, but what brings you so far from home?" asked Elsie. Katie was making her way from the kitchen, as Michael Maguire climbed out of the back of the wagon. "Michael," asked Elsie, "are you all right? You've an odd grin on your face, like the cat that ate the farmer's mice...." Elsie froze when she saw her.

"'Tis Tara Ma," her daughter said as she stepped into view. "I'm home," she cried.

Elsie dropped the towel she was holding in her hands, and said in a voice choked with emotion, "My God, is it really you?" She advanced toward her daughter, but her movements were numb. She felt like she was floating. "Tara, you've grown so tall...and lovely." The women fell into each other's arms weeping tears of joy. "When I left you in Ireland fourteen months ago," she said sobbing, "you were but a child. Now you've grown into a young woman. I cannot believe 'tis really you."

From the barn, Uncle Pat heard the commotion, and walked over to the group with Robert and Joseph at his heels. "Tara!" the boys shouted in unison as they ran to hug their sister. They nearly knocked her over as they tumbled into her arms.

"Robbie! Joseph! Look at how big you are!" It was true. When the twins had left Ireland they had been only nine. But now, the ten-year-old brothers were nearly eye-level with their sister, and it was clear that they were going to be tall like their father.

Diane looked up from her place by the wash basket at the stranger causing everyone to become so upset. She started crying, but Michael was already making his way toward her. He picked her up and laughed, "Don't cry, little one. Come and meet your big sister, Tara."

"You don't remember me do you?" asked Tara

Diane shyly pressed her cheek against her father's chest, and studied the pretty stranger.

"How old are you?"

Diane held up three fingers and everyone laughed.

Katie invited Tara and her fiends into the parlor for a pot of tea and the hot soda bread she had just pulled from the oven.

"I've dreamed of the taste of Granny Cassie's soda bread," said Tara.

"Her recipe was the best in Cootehill," Katie beamed at the compliment.

Bridget and Sean visited for an hour, but said they needed to leave. "We'll be going to stay the night at our oldest son's farm," explained Bridget. Their son lived with his wife and three children on some land located five miles south of Uncle Pat and Aunt Katie.

"We can't thank you enough for bringing our little girl home to us," said Elsie. "'Tis a fine thing you've done."

"'Twas our pleasure," said Sean. "Tara's a credit to your family. She and her friends have had quite an ordeal. You'll have much to catch up on, and we've had the fortune to hear about their adventures these past two days. We'll be seeing you in a few weeks at the barn raising, and we can catch up on how they're settling in," he added.

The story of the journey took hours in the telling, but no one could leave the parlor until the entire tale was told. Each of the friends took part in sharing their amazing adventure. Tara passed the Emerald Bottle around the room as she spoke of the many ways it had helped them along their way. It was well past midnight, and the little ones had long since gone to bed when the story of the incredible journey came to an end.

"John, Danny and Shauna," said Michael, "Elsie and I welcome you into our hearts as part of our family. You've done a great service in helping our daughter come home to us. I hope you might consider settling here. We'll do all we can to help."

"We've all had our share of sorrows in the past few years," said Danny, "but I think our troubles are behind us now. I know that, I, for one, am going to stay. I'd like to start a livestock farm that specializes in raising thoroughbred horses. When I'm makin' a decent living, I'd like to marry and have lots of children." Danny looked over at Shauna as he spoke. The trip over had changed him, as it had changed them all. He had more confidence, and when he looked at Shauna, it was she who blushed.

"I don't know what I'm going to do," offered John. "I've no knowledge of farming, but I like the idea of owning my own land. I want to write to Mam, and tell her that we've arrived safely. I told her that I would send her word through Jack and Rita in Dublin. She usually sees them three to four times during the year. I want to stay here for a while, at least, and after that...I'll do what feels right in my heart. Mam always taught me to put great stock in my instincts. I guess I'll just have to wait and see what my destiny will be." He shrugged and looked over to where Tara was sitting.

"That's grand, lads, but what about you, Shauna?" asked Katie.

"I guess I'll seek employment as a maid or a nanny somewhere. After working for the squire, I know I could work anywhere."

Katie looked over at Pat. He nodded his head and smiled. "Pat and I have always longed for children of our own, but 'twas just not meant to be. We have a lot of room here, Shauna, and 'twould be an honor if you might consider staying here with us. I'm getting on in years and could use the extra help. We'll pay you the same salary that you made at the estate, and we can guarantee the workload will not be as demanding. Michael and Elsie will be moving into their own place soon, and the house will seem so empty without them," she added sadly.

"Thank you. Your offer is most kind, and I know I would be of help to you," proclaimed Shauna. "'Tis my hope, I can save enough money to bring Ma, Billy and Mary over from Ballybay some day on a proper ship…and not in steerage."

"Our trip across the Atlantic was so easy, Ma," said Tara sadly. "I'm sorry that your voyage was wrought with trouble. I still miss Granny Cassie and think of her every day. It's strange, but I know she was with me on this journey. She helped bring me to you. I believe she placed me under that window so I could hear the evil deeds the butler and the squire were plotting."

Tara had not noticed that Shauna and Danny had slipped out of the room while she was talking. When they re-entered the parlor they walked over to where Tara sat near her mother. They each handed her a bundle that had been painstakingly wrapped tightly with cloth. "What's this?" she asked.

"Why don't you open them and see," instructed Shauna.

Tara was perplexed. She began the tedious process of unwrapping one of the bundles. It was not easy because so many layers of cloth had been wound tightly about the object.

When the task was complete, she sat staring at Granny Cassie's Belleek pitcher. She was almost too emotional to speak. "How…how?"

"The morning I searched the butler's office and found the silver vase they had accused you of stealing," began Shauna, "I happened to also see Granny Cassie's Belleek pitcher and bowl. Danny and I had already made the decision that we'd be leavin' the estate after I confronted Mary about her false testimony. We had to get to Dublin to warn you, and on impulse, I just took your pitcher and bowl. Danny and I carefully packed them in cloth, and we each carried one in our things. Some may call it stealing, but I felt justified in taking the Belleek. I reasoned that the squire and the butler had not played fair with you. You were promised passage to North America after a year of service. They not only broke their promise to you, but they were planning to keep you in servitude under false accusations.

"Please don't think harshly of me, Tara," implored Shauna, "I know that you're an honest girl and would never have taken them yourself. I agonized over this for weeks, but I've come to terms with my actions. I truly feel that what I took rightfully belonged with your family. Danny and I decided not to give them to you until you reached home. I hope you feel we did the right thing."

No one spoke for a few seconds, and when Tara looked up from the Belleek there were tears in her eyes. "Shauna, do not be hard on yourself," said Tara thoughtfully. "Sometimes I would clean the butler's office, and I would cradle the pitcher to me. It broke my heart that Granny Cassie had to part with it. In holding it, I felt that a part of her was with me."

Tara faced her parents. "I completed an honorable year of service for Squire Dellamort and Nevil Hawkins. I worked very hard to honor my family, and to repay the debt that they so cruelly extracted with sinister pleasure, not only from me, but from all the workers on the estate. When they accused me of stealing, they took my honor. There are some in Cootehill who may never know the truth."

Shauna interjected. "Mrs. Larkin knows the truth, and I've a feeling that, by now, most of the people in the village know too," she said laughing.

"I'm glad to have Granny Cassie's Belleek back, and I thank both of you for carrying it all this way for me. Aunt Katie, with your permission, I'd like to put Granny Cassie's pitcher and bowl and the Emerald Bottle in your glass china cabinet. They'll be safe there." Katie smiled and nodded her head. "When our house is finished, the Belleek, Takis and Anaki's cedar basket, and the Emerald Bottle will be displayed in a place of honor to remind us of our incredible journey."

Bailey came over and jumped on Tara's lap. "You're probably tired boy, aren't you? I don't think I would have made it through the past year without you, laddy." Tara looked around the room at her beloved family and friends. "I guess we're all a little tired. But we're here together, and tomorrow we'll begin a new journey to discover what the future holds for us on this beautiful island."

Epilogue ~ July 1853 - Maguire Farm

"They're coming, Tara!" shouted eight-year-old Diane with excitement. "I can see them coming up the road!" Diane waited on the front porch for Ma and Tara to join her.

Tara and Elsie stepped out the front door of their home, built by the family in 1849, to see Michael bringing the visitors up the long drive that led to the Maguire farm in his wagon. The three Maguire women waved eagerly in the direction of the group.

As the newcomers approached the house they saw, from a distance, a modest white two-story wooden structure. Two red brick chimneys framed the sides of the house, and smoke could be seen trailing upward into the sky from one of them. On the upper story, set into a steeply pitched roof made of wooden shingles, Irish lace curtains flapped gently in the open Dormer windows, which had been trimmed in dark green paint. Steps led up to a large white porch that framed the front of the house. An old rocker and some chairs rested there near a small table. A small black and white dog stood at the edge of the porch near the steps. Its ears were cocked as it eyed the approaching wagon. Below the steps of the porch, planters containing brightly colored flowers and a neat green lawn bordered the home, lending a charming air to the overall picture.

The convoy of visitors moved closer to the house. From her vantage point on the front seat of the wagon, the arriving guest surveyed the three women as the vehicle meandered up the drive. "That's my lovely Elsie, said Michael, "in the blue flowered dress and white apron."

The young girl sitting next to Michael, on the seat of the wagon, observed a graceful woman with dark brown hair streaked with gray waving happily at the approaching wagon. The visitor smiled and waved back at her.

"That's my daughter, Tara, wearing the purple skirt and lavender blouse. She's the one who answered your advertisement in the newspaper," said Michael. "We are very happy and excited for Tara. She is engaged to marry a fine young man this August. You'll meet him tonight. He is over at St. Teresa's church with my two boys helping Father McKenna set up for a potluck supper.

As the wagon pulled closer to the house, the guest beheld a striking young woman of eighteen with long black hair and features resembling her father. Tara wore her hair pulled back from her face and tied with an emerald green ribbon fastened into a bow at the back of her head. The young visitor observed that Tara was tall and slim. The rosy glow of her complexion set off her blue eyes and the smattering of freckles that fell across her nose. The youthful guest was immediately drawn to the warmth that radiated from Tara's expression.

"And that little imp is my youngest daughter, Diane. She's eight and keeps us all hopin' with her lively antics," added the Papa with pride.

"Y'all have a wonderful place here, Mr. Maguire, and a handsome family. I can feel that there's love in this home. We are mighty grateful for this invitation to come to your farm. I'll look forward to the two weeks I will be spendin' with your family until I must get back to New York, and resume my work on the Underground Railroad."

"Please, Esther, call me Michael. 'Twas Tara's idea to answer your advertisement, but we are all appreciative to you for bringing us some workers who can help on the farm. The cash crops from the potatoes, the oats, and the barley have brought in a good living wage for us all. We are excited to expand the planting to twenty more acres, and the help from your workers is gratefully appreciated. The boys and I worked all spring and summer, in the evenings after supper, to get their lodgings ready, and we hope they'll find them suitable."

"After what they've been through, I know that they are just happy to be workin' for folks that are goin' to treat them right, and pay them for the work they'll be doin' for y'all, Mr. Maguire...I mean Michael."

The wagon pulled to a stop in front of the house. Tara walked down the steps to shake hands with a beautiful young half-caste Negro girl with skin the shade of a pecan shell. "Welcome to our home, Esther. 'Tis, finally, so nice to meet you after all our correspondence by mail. 'Tis difficult for me to believe that you are only seventeen-years-old. I must say, I was startled when you told me so. In your letters, you expressed the wisdom of someone who seemed so much older."

The girl standing before Tara was not tall, but she stood proudly erect, as she grasped Tara's hands in both of hers. Esther had the bearing of someone who was very purposeful in her intentions. Although she was delicate in her features, she had a strong jaw line and penetrating green eyes flecked with golden dots. Tara observed that Esther's light brown hair was worn up and tied inside a brightly colored scarf of gold and red. Traces of soft wispy brown curls, streaked with strands of gold, framed a pair of the most unusual large green eyes that Tara had ever seen. The beautiful green eyes twinkled as Esther smiled. The visitor wore a light brown skirt and a red blouse, which suited her skin color perfectly. Tara liked her immediately. "Please, all of you, come in and get out of the sun," implored Tara. "We'll make our introductions after you've had a chance to get the dust off your clothes and out of your eyes."

Michael helped the new employees off the back of the wagon. All were freed dark-skinned slaves from the southern part of the United States. The two powerfully built men, two women and one young girl all looked a little nervous and uneasy as they followed the family into the house.

Elsie showed the visitors where they might freshen up as Tara and Diane finished laying out a tray, filled with tea, sandwiches, and a raisin cake, for their company. "I can't believe they're finally here," exclaimed Diane, "and that I'll have someone my own age to become friends with."

Tara smiled as she looked at her sister. Diane was growing into a pretty young girl with long blond hair and alert green eyes. *Green eyes are so rare, and yet I've seen two sets of them this morning.* She patted Diane on the head. "I'm glad that you're happy to have a new friend, Diane," said Tara.

Tara remembered the letters that she and Esther had exchanged after Tara's initial response to the newspaper ad. Esther sought employment for a group of freed slaves that she had helped flee from Louisiana on a system known as the Underground Railroad. Tara knew that the system consisted of a network of escape routes that intertwined through houses and secret hideouts up to the northern states of America and Canada.

Tara had learned in Esther's letters that the United States Congress had passed the Compromise of 1850 to pacify personal differences on the slave issue between the southern and northern states. She told Tara that the Fugitive Slave Law enticed corrupt slave catchers and private citizens to kidnap runaway slaves and freed slaves from the north, and sell them back into bondage in the south. Esther explained that the only safe place for freed slaves and escaped slaves brought up from the south was in Canada or to the south in Mexico.

When the sandwiches were laid out in the parlor, Elsie asked, "How was your trip from New York, Esther?"

"We are mighty happy to get to this place and rest a bit," said Esther sitting in a small club chair near the front window of the parlor. Bailey jumped up and settled on her lap the minute he heard the young lady speak.

"Bailey!" scolded Tara.

Esther raised her hand to signal that she did not mind the dog's presence.

"I think you've made a new friend, Esther," teased Tara. "Bailey appears to have taken a special liking to you!"

Esther replied, "I like dogs, and they continually seem to like me. We always had them on the plantation, and I've met plenty of them traveling through the swamps and trails up north. Dogs can be a slave-runner's worst terror," she shuddered.

"We are special pals aren't we, Bailey." Esther stroked and petted the dog as she spoke of their journey to the island. "We have traveled a colossal long way from New York to get here, but that was nothin' compared to comin' up from the south. Let me make the formal introductions."

"This big fella here. He's called Big Jim."

Tara thought that Big Jim was about the same size as Jack Harte. Earlier, she'd watched him bend over, so his head wouldn't hit the top of the doorway when he entered the parlor.

Big Jim stood up and made his way around the parlor shaking everyone's hand. A huge smile raked across his face as he nodded his head in greeting. Esther continued the introductions. "This other tall handsome man is called Toby." Toby also politely followed Big Jim's example and shook hands with everyone. "The two ladies are Harlene…she's Toby's wife, and this is Kitty. Kitty jumped over the broom to marry Big Jim 'bout two years ago." The ladies also stood up and politely made their way around the room to shake everyone's hand. "This precious little girl...well, she's called Sarah." Sarah, who looked to be about seven, rose and curtsied shyly.

Diane got up and walked over to where Sarah stood and asked, "Please, won't you come and sit next to me, Sarah?" A big smile overtook Sarah's face as she took Diane's hand. The two walked over and settled on the carpet near a low table that was laden with the tea and sandwiches.

The afternoon was spent getting acquainted and reviewing the terms of the agreement for wages and days off. "When we worked on dat plantation in d'south," said Big Jim, "we be working from sun up to sun down. Dere be no wages and no days off," he laughed, "so dis arrangement seem mighty fine to us, Mr. Mike."

"Well, that *is* wonderful. Why don't you all come to the cottage and see where you will be living? I think you'll like it. There's a nice sized kitchen where you ladies will be able to cook some fine meals...." Michael's voice trailed off as he led the four employees to inspect their new quarters. It had been decided that the group would rest up that afternoon and drive over to the parish church called St. Teresa for a potluck supper.

"Come up to my room, Sarah," pleaded Diane, "and see where I sleep." Sarah looked at Esther for permission, and Esther nodded her head and smiled.

"It sure is powerfully nice of you folks to take Sarah, too. She never knew her Mama and Papa. They got sold to different plantations when she was just a tot. She lived with a cranky old slave woman who took care of all the young children until they became old enough to work in the fields. Her life's been very hard. Sarah grew mighty attached to Toby and Harlene on the trip north. She was supposed to stay at the orphanage in New

York, but they decided it wouldn't be right to leave her behind."

"'Tis our pleasure to take her into our family with the others," said Elsie. "She'll start school in the fall with Diane and learn to read and write."

"That's wonderful news, ma'am. I was taught to read and write by a kindly man known on our plantation as Old Jed. Before my friend Bucky and I escaped from our plantation in Maryland, Old Jed taught us in secret at what he called Night School. What he did was for us was very dangerous because it's against the law for slaves to learn to read.

"I continued my education in New York. I have always had a hankerin' to learn, and I still am learnin'. When I'm not readin', I'm drawin'. It's a gift given to me by the Lord. That special gift used to get me in a pack of trouble as a child," Esther shared.

"Once, the plantation overseer whipped me when he caught me drawin' a picture on an old plank of wood. It was that incident with the drawing, however, that motivated me to escape slavery and become a conductor on the Underground Railroad like an esteemed woman that my people call Moses. Her real name, though, is Harriet Ross Tubman."

Tara looked at Esther with admiration. "That's an amazing story. My Granny Cassie was taught to read and write in secret, in Ireland, at a place called the Hedge School. I think it must have been very much like your Night School."

"I reckon you're right." Esther glanced over at the china cabinet and then looked back at Tara. "Y'all are doin' a fine thing for these folks. You're givin' 'em a chance to be free."

"We're happy that we can help them. Believe me, Esther, we Irish understand the struggle to be free. The troubles of your people are not so unlike our own in Ireland," said Tara wistfully.

"Excuse me for changing the subject so abruptly, folks, but I am intrigued by a piece in your china cabinet. If I'm not being too bold," inquired Esther, "I'm compelled to ask about that beautiful green bottle in the cabinet. There's just something about it that makes me think it is the prettiest thing I've ever seen."

Tara looked over at the bottle resting in the glass enclosed china cabinet built by Michael and the boys three years ago. The cabinet was home to the family's most prized possessions—the Emerald Bottle, a birch basket, and Grandma Cassie's Belleek pitcher and bowl. A chill rippled through Tara's body. She stood up, walked over to the case, slowly opened the door, and pulled the bottle from its shelf. What she saw made her tremble. Tara brought the bottle to where Esther sat and tenderly placed it in her hands. Tara returned to her seat on the sofa next to her mother. Elsie reached for her daughter's hand.

Esther looked down at the bottle and smiled. "I can't be explainin' the way I feel, but this beautiful bottle gives me a powerful feeling of love. For the first time in many months, I don't feel as burdened as I have been. In fact, I feel very much at peace. I think, however, I'm ready to take that nap you offered me before, so I'll be rested before we go to the church tonight.

Esther handed the bottle back to Tara. Elsie and Tara looked at the Emerald Bottle, mixed with the other shades of green and gold, and noticed an almost imperceptible change in its color. It was very subtle, but there was no mistaking it was there.

"Let me show you to your room, Esther," said Tara as she escorted Esther out of the parlor and up the stairs to the guestroom, "and it would be my pleasure to let you keep this bottle on the bedside table while you're here. I'm so happy that you are drawn to its beauty. I must say, the bottle has given me and my family an enormous amount of joy in the five years it has been in our possession."

Saint Teresa's hall was crowded with people from the parish who had gathered for the potluck supper and dance, but who also were filled with curiosity about the new arrivals to the island. Most had never seen a dark-skinned person before and were curious about the Maguire's new help. After the supper and most of the visiting was done, the men and children cleared a space on the floor for people to dance. A raised platform acted as a makeshift stage and held a group of local musicians who had played at the parish functions for years. A piano player, two fiddlers, and a woman who played the tambourine and spoons began the music, and the dancing commenced with a flourish. The music was the familiar Irish folk music that had been enjoyed in the old country. It was lively, and many of the dances formed into squares to repeat the same steps that had been danced in Ireland generations ago.

Tara was always happy to visit with Shauna and Danny, and these church socials provided her an occasional opportunity to catch up with her dear friends. She had not seen much of them since they had married and moved to Danny's thoroughbred farm near Covehead two summers ago. Danny's farm was prospering, and he had gained quite a reputation for breeding some of the finest horses on the island. "You look grand, Shauna," said Tara. "Let me hold little Dennis for a wee bit. My, he's a strong lad for seven months!" She held Shauna in her gaze. "You look happy, my friend."

"I am, Tara, and happy to have gotten my figure back so that I'll do you proud as your matron of honor next month. 'Tis a grand wedding it will be, for certain!"

"How's your Ma, and Billy and Mary?"

"They're fine, Tara. Thank you for askin'. They love the island as much as we do. Look at Ma dancing with Mr. McManus. I think he is daft in love with her, for sure. I'm glad though. 'Tis about time that she enjoyed some happiness again after losing Da."

At that moment, a tall dark-haired man began to make his way over to the young ladies. He had a commanding presence about him, and others in the room glanced in his direction to smile or nod their heads. Although he was only twenty-two years of age, he had been recently persuaded by the community to represent them as a member of the Legislative Council. He won the election by a landslide and pledged to work on behalf of the farmers as Minister of Agriculture. Some folks tried to engage him in conversation, and although he stopped to shake their hands and say a word or two, his eyes never left the face of the one person in the room he longed to be with. Many folks were congratulating him on the recent witty remarks he had made in the Legislature, which had been quoted in the newspaper, *The Examiner*, for its humor.

During a debate in the House, one of its members had made a derogatory remark about the Irish. It angered the young politician, and he had replied, "This man who made such a statement about the Irish is not fit to carry guts to a bear." The house called him to order and asked him to retract the statement because they did not want it to appear in the records of the Legislature. The young man agreed to retract his statement and said. "Gentlemen, I retract that statement and say: The Honorable Gentleman *is* fit to carry guts to a bear." Although the legislators laughed, they had not been pleased with the witty retort. But, according to the editor of the newspaper, Edward Whelan, the House had to accept his statement, and the quote was recorded for historical record.

At length, the young man finally stood next to the young woman he had been moving toward since entering the room. He addressed her friend congenially. "Shauna, you look positively blooming tonight, but might I steal my fiancée away from you for a quick dance? I see Danny coming this way, and he'll be wantin' to dance with you too, no doubt."

Shauna laughed at the tall captivating politician, whose friendship she held so dearly. "Stop with your blarney, Councilman."

Tara looked into the man's eyes and smiled. "You may be able to charm half the population of this island with your smooth words, John Martin Corcoran. But remember, Shauna and I knew you when you were just a bold lad of sixteen who could juggle five pine cones while spinning a good yarn about your escapades as a Tinker," laughed Tara.

"Sshhh lass, now don't you be giving away all my talents so freely," John whispered. He lifted young Dennis out of Tara's arms and kissed the baby on the forehead, like a good politician. "Poor, wee lad looks too much like his Da."

"I heard that remark, my friend," said Danny as he plucked the baby from John's arms.

The couple made a fine pair, as they whirled about the dance floor to the rhythm of a waltz. "'Tis a fine thing you did bringing those people to the island, Tara. 'Twill be good for your Da's farm, and 'twill be good for them. I had a long talk with Esther. She's a remarkable young woman. You know, in many ways she reminds me a lot of you." John looked into Tara's eyes and smiled. "You possessed a wisdom and tenacity that far exceeded your years. After she settles Sarah and the others here, she told me she'll join a Quaker family who'll help her on her next trip south. As soon as she gets back to New York, she'll travel to Maryland to bring a group of slave children up north from her old plantation. Through messages, sent along the Underground Railroad network, she knows they're already in serious danger. The path that Esther has chosen is very risky work, and yet, she's committed to the task. She feels it's her destiny to help others who long to be free from the tyranny of slavery. I like her, Tara. I like her very much."

"She has found the bottle, John. Or perhaps I should say that the bottle has found her. 'Tis beginning to change in color." John stared at Tara through wide eyes, too stunned to speak. "The bottle will help her on her journey, John. I'm certain of that."

"How do you feel about losing it after all this time?"

Tara sighed. "I'm happy 'twas mine for a while, but I'm glad if it'll help others find their way to safety, my love." Tara looked up into the violet blue eyes of the man she would marry in August, five years to the day that they had arrived on the island to begin a new life. She and John had been separated for much of that time while he had been away from the island working and furthering his education. They had seen each other from time to time, but she was pursuing a degree in botany. It was not until he had come back to the island to settle, a year ago, that he had fallen completely in love with the young girl whom he had helped journey home to the family she loved so much.

Diviña was healthier than ever, and surprised the couple by saying that she would come for their wedding in August. The odd thing was the timing of her announcement. Her letter had been post marked the very day that John had asked Michael and Elsie Maguire for Tara's hand in marriage in the parlor of the Maguire home. John swore to Tara that his idea for proposing had hit him so quickly he had not had time to mention his plans to anyone.

The couple decided that they would maintain a small farm just outside of the capital city of Charlottetown to make use of Tara's skills as a botanist. Although the famine in Ireland had been over for two years, she wanted to work on ways to improve germination of the seed potato, and study crop insects in the hope that a blight of that magnitude might never happen again.

"You look beautiful tonight, Tara," said John.

"A lot different from the scrawny little girl you took to find her parents five years ago." Tara laughed.

"Well, I think down deep, I had feelings for that scrawny little girl who was much wiser than her years, even then," he confessed.

"And I looked up to the tall handsome boy who gave up his whole world for me."

"After all we've been through together, Tara, it's hard to imagine that the rest of our lives could match the adventure of that journey, but I am sure it will. By the way, I had word from Josh and Lisa. They'll be sailing on the *Lisa Renee* with the three boys and little Avery Victoria, so they can join us for our wedding in August. 'Tis turning out to be quite the celebration. Personally, I can't wait for the day to arrive."

"'Twill mark the beginning of the first day of the rest of our lives together, my love, and that will begin a whole new journey for us," said Tara as John whirled her around the dance floor.

Tara's intuition had been correct. The bottle, entrusted to her by Diviña those fateful years ago, had begun to change color on the day of Esther's arrival. Over the next few weeks, Tara had many long talks with Esther to explain all that she knew about the mysteries and powers of the bottle. Gradually the shades of green were replaced with splashes of copper and bronze, intermingled with shades of ebony and specks of gold.

Parting with the beautiful emerald treasure that had helped her find her way home to her family, was bittersweet for Tara. She was happy that the bottle had found another person to help on a new adventure, but it was like losing an old friend. Tara wondered if Diviña had felt the same emotions when she'd entrusted the bottle to her.

At the end of two weeks, Esther announced that it was time for her to sail back to New York to resume her work on the Underground Railroad. Tara and John, accompanied by Bailey, drove her to Charlottetown where a steamship waited to take her back to her work in the United States. There, the friends spoke fond farewells.

Esther smiled at her new friends. "There are a lot of folks who need help to find their way north and to good people like you. I want to thank you for your kindness in having me these past weeks. I feel more rested and unburdened than I have in a very long time. I'm refreshed, and feel oddly confident that I can face the difficult times I know lie ahead. Thanks for welcoming all of us into your home. Big Jim, Kitty, Toby and Harlene are very happy to be here. They feel safe. I think young Sarah is happiest of all," she added warmly.

"We feel blessed to have them. Already, they've been a big help to Da and the boys."

Esther spoke in reverent tones. "Mostly, I want to thank you for giving me the bottle, and the clever little pouch that will help me in my travels. Somehow, I feel the bottle will give me the strength to make the journey south, at least one more time." Esther sighed as if reflecting on the enormous task before her.

"Place your trust in the bottle, and it will guide you on this journey, Esther. It will help you, as it helped me," said Tara earnestly.

Esther presented Tara and John with two thin packages wrapped in brown paper. "I made this little wedding gift for y'all," she added softly.

Whenever Esther spoke of her work on the Underground Railroad she seemed wise beyond her years, but now, she looked timid and vulnerable as she spoke. It was as though she was but a small child of ten, and not the young woman who was off to rescue enslaved children. "I hope you'll find a spot to put them in your new home as a remembrance of our time together," she uttered with endearing sincerity.

Slowly, Tara unwrapped the first package to reveal a framed portrait about twelve inches tall and ten inches wide. It was a detailed drawing, in black ink, of Tara sitting near a stream with Bailey on her lap. The wind blew gently against her hair and onto a face that was smiling as she looked into the distance, as if pondering the future. It was a remarkable likeness that captured the spirit of the girl and her dog.

"I don't remember when you could have done this, Esther. 'Tis so lovely, and I'm moved to tears at the beauty of your talent. Thank you so much." Tara passed the drawing to John and stepped forward to hug Esther.

"You have an incredible gift," murmured John, who was admiring the picture.

The other package was an oil painting done on canvas. Tara looked at the colorful painting and gasped. "I cannot believe that you could have painted this…why…'tis perfect! What you have captured in this painting…is…the truth."

It was the bottle, exactly as it had been before it began its transformation to the way it looked now at Esther's side. The Emerald Bottle, mixed with the other shades of green and gold, was infused with a light that seemed to radiate in all directions. The painting preserved the perfect image of the bottle, which had captured the true essence of Tara's spirit.

"I am overcome with emotion. These two works of art will hold a place of honor in our home. You're a remarkable woman, Esther, and we'll never forget you. Our home will always be open to you," whispered Tara in soft tones, as she held the painting to her heart.

"Take care of Tara, John. She's a rare treasure," counseled Esther.

"I'm a lucky man, Esther. I promise that I'll love and honor her all my life," said John as he gathered Tara affectionately to his side.

Esther boarded the ship that would carry her to New York. She leaned over the side-rail to wave to the handsome pair, standing on the dock, holding a black and white dog and the gifts she had made to celebrate the joy of their upcoming wedding. The cherished bottle, hung near Esther's right side by a strap that fastened across her left shoulder. It was the same leather pouch that had been made for Tara by Diviña.

Esther waved one last time. She cradled the leather pouch, which encased the mysterious Bronze Bottle in her arms. The gesture seemed to give her an added measure of strength. Standing a little taller, she lifted her chin, took in a deep breath, and smiled one last time at the couple, with a warmth that emanated from deep inside her.

As the ship pulled out of the harbor, it marked the beginning of a voyage that would take the new owner of the bottle to a group of young slave children held in bondage. With the assistance of a young Quaker family, Esther would guide the children on a dangerous journey north. A journey that, hopefully, would lead the children to freedom.

* * * * * *

Author's Note: The historical facts featured in *The Emerald Bottle* are research-based. Belleek, however, did not actually begin production until 1849 when John Caldwell Bloomfield inherited the Castlecaldwell estate, in the village of Belleek, from his father. Mindful of plight of his tenants during the potato famine, he wanted to provide them with some form of worthwhile employment.

CPSIA information can be obtained
at www.ICGtesting.com
Printed in the USA
BVHW031519150720
583805BV00001B/91